WHERE ARE THE HEROES?

Stephanie Bradley

Published by Xlibris Corporation
International Plaza II, Suite 340
Philadelphia PA 19113
Copyright © 2006

Cover Graphic Design: Linda Suffidy

Library of Congress Control Number: 2005910322
ISBN 10:   Hardcover   1-4257-0371-2
                      Softcover   1-4257-0370-4

ISBN 13:   Hardcover   978-1-4257-0371-4
                      Softcover   978-1-4257-0370-7

This is a work of fiction. Names, characters, places and incidents either are the product of
the author's imagination or are used fictitiously, and any resemblance to any actual persons,
living or dead, events, or locales is entirely coincidental.

This book was printed in the United States of America.

31985

CONTENTS

Prologue   7

The Arrest   13

Prison 535   40

The Republic   69

The Event   106

The New Republic   140

The Interrogation   177

Epilogue   213

For Hannah

The standing army is only an arm of the standing government. The government itself, which is the only mode, which the people have chosen to execute their will, is equally liable to be abused and perverted before the people can act through it.

—Thoreau

PROLOGUE

Dear reader,

I hope that this book finds you well and the things that have been turned upside down have now been placed upright again. I don't have a name; no one does. That interpersonal familiarity stopped a year and a half ago as a form of self-protection against the growing surveillance that pervaded the Republic in the years after the great catastrophe.

Since the adoption of the universal surveillance procedures by the administration, thousands of people have been identified as terrorists using the toll-free antiterrorist hotline my staff implemented. Within minutes of being identified, these people are arrested and subsequently executed for crimes against the Republic.

The policy was initially intended as a way to stop the spread of terrorism in the Republic by the accused immigrants. In its original form it only had the authority to arrest and detains all immigrants. When the attacks kept occurring the legislation was amended to include the immediate arrest and death for all immigrants residing in the borders of the Republic.

However, far from assuaging the citizens concerns of another attack, the elimination of the immigrants only served to intensify the fear of attack because the only known enemy was eliminated but the fear of attack remained. As a result in the era after the completion of the immigrant pogroms and cleansing the number of calls to the antiterrorist hotline increased. The accursed were now anyone and the badge colour did not matter. Everyone was a suspect and therefore open to an anonymous terrorist tip on the buzzing hotline.

It was at this time that the people spontaneously decided to refrain from using their name in public out of this mistaken belief that they would be immune from persecution. They were wrong and now names are obsolete. The only identification currently in the Republic is the DNA number assigned to each person by the Department of Internal Republic Security.

By the time the residents recognized that there was a personal security problem, eliminating one's name was of no help. This recognition had to come earlier, and most, like me, were content to ignore it as long as they were immune from the mass military purges. Thus, when the DNA-badge legislation was expanded to include all residents, names became obsolete. All personal identification was tied to the chip and number sequence contained on the bright yellow badge all residents were required to wear on their upper right arm at all times.

Now in the Republic when a person dies, or is found dead, there is no funeral or mourning; there is only a call made to the local public health department office to sanitize the polluted area. As soon as the call is received at the department, a local sanitation unit is dispatched to the contaminated area to remove and transport the lifeless body to the department's central sanitary facilities where the corpse is deposited into the fiery mouth of the furnace and instantly devoured. Afterward, the units then leave and wait for the next call. There is no funeral and no visitation. There is only anonymity and death.

In the New Republic, a person does not exist. All that exists are numbers connected to a machine that spits out coordinates. These coordinates are used to provide instant tracking for the Internal Republic Security officials when a neighbour, friend, family member, colleague, or stranger reports a person for engaging in or planning a terrorist activity. In the New Republic, the only-recognized identities are the informants, the database. In vain, all attempt to hide from them, but none can escape their hidden and omnipresent reach.

That is why I am here. He made a call to the Department of Internal Republic Security hotline to report me for seditious and unlawful public conduct. Within twenty minutes of the call, I was efficiently removed from the world and incarcerated at prison 535. During my stay here, I have been brutally tortured, denigrated, starved, and held without the prospect of bail, a lawyer, or a trial. My fate was pronounced the minute the call was made, and there is no opportunity for an appeal. I have had my interrogation and now am waiting for the moment that I will be blindfolded, gagged, and transported to the prison crematorium where I will be devoured and vanished in the licking flames like the many others who preceded me here.

However, dear reader, unlike the others who were tortured and executed before me, I am a special case. Not only am I the first to request and survive the interrogation instead of accepting the offer of assisted suicide after repeated bodily mutilation by the guards, I am the first legitimate prisoner to be housed at the illustrious facility. Unlike the countless others before me, the charges against me are true.

I am prisoner GT90347. It is the same number I wore on my badge before my arrest. Now it is prominently displayed in on the upper chest area of the right hand side of my orange jumpsuit placed on me by the warden after my official decree of guilt several days ago—at least it seems like days.

In reality I don't know how long I have been here. The days seem to blend seamlessly into the next. One moment I was surrounded by complete darkness, the next glaring lights, then loud unbearable music followed by a trip to the pre-interrogation torture chamber where my body and mind are subjected to endless and unimaginable acts of pain and torture.

I also don't know how long they are going to keep me here before my execution, but the longer the wait, the more I get to write; and that makes the wait a lot more bearable.

I am able to write because of my previous special status in the Republic. The interrogator, my former supervisor, against the wishes of the warden, permitted my request to have a small computer delivered to my cell under the auspices of playing games. He knew I often enjoyed a good game of online cards or chess before an important meeting to clear my mind, but somehow I think he knew the real reason for my request.

I was surprised that he agreed to my request; but knowing him, I know there must be some twisted reward for him in the end, and for him there will be. He knows that I have opted to forgo the games and opted to use the word processor to write down all my regrets and misdeeds before the moment of my pending obliteration. I don't care what he knows, at least I can write.

It is amazing how quickly people can be forgotten. All the others vanished from public view the moment of their arrest. A removal effectively results in the negation of the arrested or dead person's existence. Being forgotten is the most painful price of anonymity. No one knows you, and therefore, no one cares whether you are there one day and not the next.

In the past, any person exhibiting signs of detachment and disinterest in the welfare of others and the state was diagnosed as possessing a dangerous pathological antisocial mental disorder and committed to an institution for treatment. Today it is the opposite. Today, in the Republic, any person who shows signs of individual initiative, care, and concern for others is reported, removed, imprisoned, executed, and summarily forgotten. Today there are no heroes, there are only murderers and zombies.

I knew the fear of the informant would drive people to hide and disengage from others, which in time would lead to separation and the erosion of individual identity. I knew by reading the reports and writing the policy that it is almost impossible to remember someone without a name. In fact, I should not have needed to read the reports. It was obvious, a matter of common sense, that the elimination of names would render every person's life lonely, alienated, isolated, superfluous, and, therefore, meaningless.

The sad reality is that I did not care. I did not want to reflect on the repercussions of what I was writing, all I wanted to do was complete the requirements of my job, go out, and go home. At no point in time in the early years of my directorship did I attempt to see the black hole that was forming in the Republic that like an unstoppable leviathan would rise up and devour all of the residents and the heroes with them.

In my drunken and blinded state I thought I was a hero. With my policy and legislation I thought that I was standing up and slaying the dragons of oppression against all adversity to save the Republic. It did not occur to me that I was creating the dragon that would end up devouring all of the people brave enough to be on the dark and deserted streets until there could be no heroes because I had help create a Republic of corpses.

To have a story, there must be actors and a witness to record the words and deeds of the actors. The same is true for history. In the current carnation of the Republic, there is no history because there are no people to act, and there are no witnesses to record and tell the stories of the actors' deeds. Even a tyrant needs a witness and author to broadcast his enterprise of seduction and intention in the form of words.

This fact makes my writing difficult. I am constrained by numbers and pronouns. However, regardless of the constraints and my current dilapidated condition I am determined to write the sad tale and attempt to restore the possibility for history and other stories. I apologize that I am its author, but I assure the reader that I have concealed no crimes and added nor have I devalued any character's virtues represented in the dark book and I guarantee the reader that my memory does not deceive me. It cannot because I was a witness and active participant in all the atrocities that unfolded. As its chronicler, I promise have done my best to present an honest and accurate account of the demise of the Republic.

The purpose of this story is not to gain sympathy for me because as you will soon discover, I am vile and despicable and deserve none. It is written as an artefact to become an orphan for others to read and judge its contents and its actors and wonder how it is that it could ever have happened and to find the heroes as I go to my ashen grave.

Dear reader, my sentence is declared, and my fate is assured. I will die. That is the only conclusion to this tale that I can offer. I am isolated, mutilated, and half blind. I have no knowledge of the future. I only know the past and the past and the present and this is what I will write. I leave the future to you to determine after my bones have melted and merged with the others below me.

Sincerely,
GT90347

THE ARREST

The only justice in the story is that it will begin with my arrest and end with my death.

The arrest is important because it is illustrative of all the arrests many others have endured in the past few years since I have been the director of the Department of Internal Republic Security. My death is less important. The only irony is that as soon as I have begun to understand and appreciate life, I must die. Of course, it could have been different because everything always can, but for me, my time has expired. I only hope that this book and the reason for my arrest can help open up a new opportunity for the remaining residents living in the Republic from the current nightmare I helped create.

My arrest was clinical. There had been so many before me that the officers had found a way to turn each arrest into an efficient and captivating drama for all remaining citizens to watch. I was arrested on Wednesday, July 22, at 3:20 p.m. I only know the time because I heard one of the officers announce it on the portable loudspeaker that pierced through the deafening din of the super sleek black choppers that were circling above the five-hundred-acre wooded park.

I must admit that despite being fully away of the outcome of my actions when I first heard and saw the mass onslaught of tactical choppers I was a bit surprised. I had allowed myself to get caught up in the moment of the commission of my crime that I temporarily forgot what year it was or that he was waiting their patiently to issue my death warrant. This is why within seconds after digesting the reality of my impending arrest, I began to experience great waves of regret—regret that I was unable to complete my speech and distribute more pamphlets before the officers arrived. If only I had started sooner, but it was already too late.

My plan was all about timing and numbers. I had the numbers but was uncertain as to the timing. I knew beforehand that the length of my dissent was out of my control, but I was still a little disappointed with myself. I should have known that he would arrange my arrest before I would be satisfied or achieve my objective. Life in the Republic was up to his discretion and all actions for his amusement.

However, I also knew that there was one outstanding factor that was somewhat out of both of our control, and that was the media—at least until he sent the message to have the coverage cancelled and all records of it erased. Once I completed this thought process, I dropped the rest of the pamphlets, pressed send on my hand-sized computer, then stood still to brace myself for the coming impact.

The months leading up to my arrest had marked a significant reduction in the frequency of the arrests. The reason for this decline was that the antiterrorist policies I drafted had been successful. The remaining residents in the Republic were terrified to be seen in public for a prolonged time out of fear of arrest. As a result, they stayed in their homes and avoided all human contact.

I knew he was happy about this, but I wasn't. I missed seeing people holding hands, smiling, walking in groups so engaged in conversation that the sidewalk was blocked. Instead, the streets had become completely derelict and deserted. The world of the Republic had become a virtual wasteland and concrete graveyard. Even with the immunity my position granted me I did not want to be outside longer than necessary. I got tired of seeing people pass by with their heads down and with vacant and sullen expressions on their once-exuberant faces.

Mostly, however, I hated having to see and step over the scattered bodies lying in strange, fantastic poses with bowed shoulders, bent knees, heads thrown back, chins pointing upward, and eyes wide open depicting the inner fear of their impending death for having forgotten to wear their legislated DNA badge. Remembering that and the sticky red trail of blood that splattered and stained the white concrete makes me shudder. How correct my housemate was before she too died.

Initially the terror evoked by the arrest was so great that the sheer horror of them always resulted in large crowds of people at each arrest site. As the number of arrests increased, the tactical units began to use their fame to entertain the terrified onlookers, which in effect turned the arrests into a well-honed, precise, dramatic spectacle worthy of a multimillion-dollar action movie feature.

The shrinking of people from the streets into the shadowy confines of their homes made arrest a grand spectacle. By the time of my arrest, the action, lights, and suspense the seizures engendered made the frequent arrests become one of the primary sources of entertainment for the restrained citizens in the Republic. Thus, when the number of arrests began to decline, several people began to use the terrorist-prevention hotline to lodge an accusation against a local pedestrian or colleague for the mere entertainment of watching the dramatic and action-packed explosive procedure.

Admittedly the arrests were quite spectacular compared to the lonely and mediocre lives most citizens experienced. During the arrests, one could see guns, choppers, armoured vehicles, elite tactical units, and a helpless reported terrorist being forcefully removed from the Republic, which enabled the otherwise paralyzed citizens to participate in an action drama that never ended.

After several years of observing and ordering the units to make the arrests, I noticed an interesting yet administratively ignored phenomenon about the arrests. The arrests had become one of the few times the registered citizens in the Republic spontaneously gathered to watch and participate in a public event.

Initially the significance of the observation eluded me until one happened outside of my condo complex. The spellbound crowd totalled nearly five thousand spectators. Only a sporting event could draw more people to congregate in an open and public location without fear of reprisal.

For some reason I never mentioned this observation to anyone. It was like my own private secret. Something I could see that no one else could. However, it is highly possible that he did too because he began to follow and talk with me more after the realization than he had ever before. It was almost as if he had found a kindred sprit, a kind of friend, but a definite threat and potential enemy to the fragile and besieged Republic.

While planning my public action, I kept this fact about numbers and spontaneous interconnectivity in mind. In fact, my entire plan was devised to achieve maximum numbers. To do so, I wanted to choose a spot that naturally had a higher population density than other areas as well as had the greatest amount of open surrounding space for bedazzled spectators to flood to and watch the action-packed arrest scene unfold. And, if I planned it right, people would be attracted to my pre-selected scene of transgression several minutes before the police units arrived to shackle and transport me to the place of my death.

More people meant more media that would translate into coverage for a week, especially given the profile of the captured criminal. He didn't mind; he was bored and wanted something exciting to watch, at least for twenty minutes. He also knew that he controlled the media and could cancel the coverage and reporting with one phone call. That is also why I had to be more prepared.

My advantage was that I knew I was going to die, so I had nothing to lose. I could go all out without fear. He, on the other hand, had everything he had worked on to lose. That knowledge is what gave me the courage to commit the felony and suffer the unrelenting consequences I endured following the perpetration of my crime. It was precisely what I wanted.

In the terrorist-arrest script, the choppers are always the first to arrive. Fifty choppers are dispatched from the central headquarters to arrest a single person. If two terrorists are reported to be acting together, the number of choppers and land personnel dispatched is doubled. This number ensures that with each arrest, the sound of the choppers arriving can be heard from nearly fifty kilometres away signalling the citizens to turn on their computers, televisions, and radios to get a live account of the proceedings.

I must say, the approach of the choppers is an ominous sound and sight. They look like a sea of large black locusts approaching, circling, and waiting to swoop down and swarm the earth.

Each chopper is dark black with a lightweight custom-made titanium frame that is easy to manoeuvre and operate. Every chopper seats eight elite tactical officers and has room for up to five prisoners to kneel on its hard floor.

The technology used in the current models is so sophisticated that the vehicle virtually flies itself. This allows the officers to dedicate more attention tracking and capturing and then torturing its passenger prisoners.

Tracing the reported terrorists is initially done through the DNA database housed in the Department of Internal Republic Security Department headquarters. In the Republic, each citizen is required to carry and prominently display the government-issued DNA badge at all times. Failure to wear the mandatory badge is punishable by immediate death. Assassinating non-badge-wearing residents is the prerogative of any citizen. When this occurs, the dead bodies are left on the street to remind the citizens of the moribund consequences of dissent. The lifeless body is then left there until it begins to decompose. At this time, the Public Health Department dispatches its sanitation unit to remove the decaying corpse from the public area and dispose of it in the local crematorium.

Citizens wearing the required badge accused of committing or conspiring to commit a crime against the Republic are to be reported using the twenty-four-hour toll-free terrorist-prevention hotline. The caller is prohibited from killing the accused because they are considered citizens of the Republic and, therefore, given the courtesy of an arrest and the option of an interrogation before being similarly disposed as the nonbadge-wearing residents.

The DNA database is activated at the time of the informant's call. The number sequence contained on the badge is entered into the lead chopper computer that is linked to the DNA database. It then sends a locator signal shown on a 360-degree real-time video camera that acts like a super-sensory bloodhound to pinpoint the exact location of the identified terrorist through the microchip contained in each badge. The coordinates from the camera then connect to the global position system map that supplies accurate location information to the flight crew on the in-flight computer.

The DNA database policy paper was drafted under my supervision as the Director of the Department of Internal Republic Security. The purpose of the legislation was to contain and eliminate terrorists living and operating in the Republic made known after the combined attacks that rocked the once-impenetrable foundation of the Republic.

The purpose of the DNA database was twofold. First, it was used to create a national database containing all the registered criminals and immigrants. Second, but equally as important as the first, it was used to provide a unique public identification for immigrants. The collected DNA is stored in the national database to compare those samples with biological evidence from the scenes of unsolved crimes for the easier resolution of future crimes and terrorist events.

To number the DNA, the scientists employed by the Department of Internal Republic Security took the four DNA nucleotides ATCG and denatured them into single strands using heat. When this process was completed they annealed a primer to one of the template strands. This primer is specifically constructed so that its 3' end is located next to the DNA sequence of interest. Either this primer or one of the nucleotides should be radioactively or fluorescent labelled so that the final product can be detected on a gel. When the primer was successfully attached to the DNA the scientist then divided the genetic solution into four tubes labelled G, A, T, and C. Once separated reagents were added to the samples to synthesize the DNA and nucleotides were inserted on to the growing chain of the DNA polymerase until dideoxynucleotides were incorporated into the chain in place of a normal nucleotide terminating the chain reaction and establishing the sequence for that DNA sample.

When the sequence was identified, the same DNA was then entered into a condo plot that displayed a unique horizontal bar for each of the sixty-four triplets of nucleotides that make up the entered DNA. The generated horizontal condo bar then enabled the criminologists to derive a unique DNA number sequence. The number was then entered into the DNA database associated with the name, country of origin, date of birth and current address, height and eye colour of the isolated individual and a badge issue with the unique DNA identifier proximately printed

Once they were registered in DNA database, the immigrants were given a blue-coloured badge displaying their DNA number that they were required to wear at all times. The badges were coloured and given to each registered immigrants to identify and segregate them from the rest of the population. Once this legislation was in place the future pogroms and liquidation strategy was easy to administer.

About one year into its implementation, the chancellor magistrate proposed the idea of extending the DNA badge and database system to everyone. In this policy, newborn infants would be automatically profiled at birth; children at school and adults were given the option of registering themselves. The overriding objective of the proposal was to produce a complete national database of all the Republic's citizens. The badge was earmarked to replace all other forms of identification and become the primary national identifier. The proposed amendment would then give a different colour of badge to the criminals and immigrants and citizens and government officials as a means of separating the citizens from the rest of the population. Anyone not wearing the badge then became a suspect for surveillance.

Not long after the promulgation of the amended DNA legislation, the feelings of insecurity and fear of attack once again began to arise. Even with the colour coding, few felt comfortable enough to distinguish who was a citizen and who was a criminal or immigrant. After the amendment was passed, a new and unprecedented form of surveillance and police control began to emerge. The badges made surveillance highly visible, created self-policing, and triggered a shift from targeting specific suspects to a categorical suspicion of everyone.

It was this last effect that led to the erosion of the use of names and the rise of perpetual fear in every town and city of the Republic. Where one was previously defined by whom one was, there was a shift to what traits one had. In this new identification system, names were not important; the only important thing was the number sequence displayed on your badge.

The tactical land-arrest units consist of fifteen four-man teams. Each team moves covertly to the specified location through the city's extensive network of streets, waterways, and sewers. The land units are instructed to only move in on the criminal/terrorist after the choppers have secured the location and sealed off possible escape routes for the captive to flee.

This was the scene at precisely 3:20 p.m. where I was standing addressing the crowd. The land units and several hundred regular officers descended on the park, closing in the large five hundred acres from all sides spraying tear gas at each step to flush out the congregated crowd and immobilize me. Snipers were also strategically stationed in the wooded area and the high-rise buildings across the street to provide fire support and conduct intelligence to the team during the operation in preparation for any possible armed resistance.

Amid the gasping, choking, vomiting, and crying from the gas that burned like lighter fluid on my skin and eyes I attempted to focus on the encroaching units. From my clouded vantage point, all I could see was a mass of nebulous black shadows moving through the dense fog.

How long would they take? I wondered. In the yellow poisoned air and laboured breathing, it seemed as if the world-renowned rapid response unit was not up to its usual blitz speed and was moving in slow motion.

Was I going to make it through until they arrived? It felt as if I would either die from affixation or burn to death slowly from the inside out.

The most disturbing thing I remember about the arrest is that despite all the commotion and the number of onlookers present, everyone remained silent. The only noise that could be heard was the constant hum of the hovering choppers, the team radio communications, the heavy breathing of the running officers, and the pounding police boots as they hit the ground in unison creating the hypnotic sound of a monotonous drum beat.

I had never been so close to an arrest before, and for a brief moment of cowardice, I wished I weren't so close then either. It felt a bit like being in a dream, but yet strangely it felt more real than anything else that had happened in the last few years since the cataclysmic event. Clad in a dark black flame-resistant uniforms, ballistic helmets and gas masks, thick bullet-resistant vests, poised handguns, and throat mikes crackling, the unidentifiable officers descended upon me like a pack of wolves upon their trapped prey.

I must have been standing when they arrived because the next thing I remembered feeling was a blow to my back from one of the unit officer's nightsticks and hitting the hard ground with a thud. When I looked up, all I could see around me was a circle of officers with their guns pointed at every portion of my body. I tried to move, but between the pain and fear, my body was frozen. All I could do was lie motionless and stare at the hidden faces that surrounded me.

Suddenly, like a jolt into consciousness, I found myself being forced upright onto my knees by a gang of gruff officers. Then I felt my hands against their will being forced behind my back and constrained by a pair of cold, biting steel handcuffs while my feet were simultaneously chained so tightly that my circulation was instantly cut off. When this occurred, I let out an instinctive moan from the piercing pain and discomfort.

My scream prompted one of the reaper masked officers to laugh and mutter, 'Don't like it, eh? Should I tighten them?' He laughed again and kicked me in the ribs to accent his authority.

The unexpected kick made me moan again, but he had already turned his attention to his colleague to temporarily save me from more forceful and injurious physical assaults.

'Perfect day for a sanitize,' he casually remarked.

'Yes. I was beginning to worry that we would not have any fun or contribute to the well-fare of the republic today.' another faceless officer replied.

The banal conversation continued, but I was unable to hear the rest of it over my own thoughts.

When I first awoke to the incessant beeping of my alarm clock set for what I consider to be the inhuman time of 7:00 a.m., I had no prior intention to implement my subversive plan. The only plan I had was to go to the office and do some more research, complete some files, and then head to the international soccer game that was scheduled to kick off after the opening at the new multi-sport stadium.

I did not have a ticket to the game because I always wait to the last minute to make decisions, but I was sure I could get one from a scalper or in the noise-bleed section. There are giant screens televising the game throughout the stadium, so I was not concerned about my seating location—although near the pitch is always better.

I like to watch soccer because it is the only time large groups of people come together and communicate, even if it is directed at a team. The other thing I enjoy about soccer is the composition of players. Most of the top teams have a roster of varying ethnicity and national identities working harmoniously together to achieve a common objective. Watching soccer is also the only time I can relax and let the demons of my day evaporate, so I did it as often as I could.

I lived alone. I used to share a flat with my old college friend, but after the immigration act and its sister database policy I was instrumental in implementing, she decided that it was best to move out. Her family had moved to the Republic fifty years ago and, under the new law, were required to register their DNA and be one of the first groups of people mandated to wear the mandated badge.

Prior to her leaving, we had a number of discussions that soon turned into heated and irresolvable arguments about the anti-constitutional merits of the legislation and the serious long-term ramifications of the policy on the fabric of the Republic. She argued in vain about the possibilities of mass purges and arrests and public persecution that would eventually occur with the introduction of the badge identification system. I argued back that she was paranoid and that the badges were to protect the innocent people and make for easier and more efficient capture of the criminals and terrorists.

I miss her a lot. She was my dearest friend and confidant. When she died, a part of me did too. In some ways, she is responsible for me being here today. I know what she would have said and done. In some way, during our discussions, I knew she was correct, but I was never one to back down on an argument, especially when I my entire department was being attacked. After she moved out, she never contacted me again.

In retrospect, she made the correct decision. If I could, I would move away from myself too. The last thing I heard about her was a memo on my desk stating that badge number XY6597 had been arrested for subterfuge and for conspiracy to commit terrorist acts upon the Republic. The next line stated the time and location of her death.

When I read the report I went temporarily numb. It was the first time I had experienced genuine emotion since she moved out. For years, I had been moved automatically through life drafting policy, hiring security forces, procuring weapons and tactical vehicles, and arranging and ordering arrests. I had ordered her arrest too. I signed on the line after the anonymous tip came in about her planned terrorist attempt to subvert the administration. I knew that this report was probably true. I also knew she was lucky to have made it that far without being executed. All her family had been eliminated a few years earlier, and after the initial set of purges, there were few people left wearing the bright, distinct immigrant badge.

The unravelling process had been gradual—so gradual that most people did not even notice that it was happening. One day, one's neighbour or colleague would just be gone. Most people arrested did not even make it into the media. The only news offered about an arrest was the purpose of the arrest and the DNA numbers of those arrested. Only I, and a few select others, knew the name and address of each person arrested and killed because my office retained all the registration records.

After reading her name and time of death on the execution report, I absently filed the report in my large cabinet and slumped into my chair at my desk and asked myself what had I done. My cabinet was full, and the arrest warrants kept coming in. I wanted to shut off the world until I realized I already had. After this realization, I sat frozen in my chair staring at the thousands of sheets of papers containing the names and personal details of all the people arrested and executed. All dead, none remembered.

My alarm clock then buzzed me back into consciousness. For those few minutes before the incessant buzz of the alarm, I had felt like I was in my office. After being abruptly pulled out of my dream, I shut off the beeping alarm. I pushed back the covers, got out of bed, and instinctively shuffled down the long dark hardwood hallway to the kitchen where I mechanically poured myself a cup of coffee and turned on the radio to listen to the morning news.

In the years following the series of cataclysmic events, I increasingly found listening to the news to be annoying. I hated its emptiness and perfunctory tone, but each morning I would habitually sit in my kitchen, drink my coffee, and listen to the drone of the announcer's voice on the early morning talk radio news.

I found the coverage the most annoying. All the news was about events. None of the news was about a person. This was the case regardless of how significant or insignificant the event was. It paid cultist homage to what was happening or what had happened but never mentioned any people or their relation to the event and presented the events as if they would naturally occur even if people weren't in the world to set the plan and set the event in motion. This is why about halfway through listening to the news, I always began to get irritated and turn off the radio before shuffling off to the office.

That morning was different. For some reason, I was not as irked with the litany of events being described. The only explanation I can conjure for my apparent tranquility was the underlying realization that I would never have to listen to the news again. I had not decided to do anything different that day, but inside I felt that there was something ideal about that day. It was nothing tangible but definitely portentous.

The internal sensation was strong enough that instead of turning off the news, I found myself straining my ears to listen to the droning broadcast. I sipped my coffee and abstractly heard something about the evening soccer game and grand opening of a suburban shopping mall. Then I heard nothing.

I can't remember if there was a pause in the broadcast or if I had gotten lost in my thoughts. All I remember was looking out the open French window watching the thin white curtains billow in the breeze and trying to discover the root of the feeling I had in the back of my head. The one thing I do remember clearly was that I was tired of thinking. I had been thinking for months since the day I stored my friend's death certificate in my office cabinet.

For months, I had been miserable I was like everyone else—an inmate in the madhouse erected and dutifully administered by policies authored by my own hand. In those months, I had felt uneasy in my own skin; but recently, the growing silence in the world had become deafening, and I could not take the silence and emptiness any longer.

'The stock market continued its meteoric rise yesterday,' the monotone voice from the radio startled and jolted me back into consciousness. 'The chancellor magistrate is . . .' I snapped and let out a low scream as I jumped from my stool, spilling coffee all over the multi-coloured ceramic-tiled floor. In my head I wanted to clean it up, but instead I just stared blankly at the floor in a half-catatonic stupor unable to move or find the energy to pick up the rag attached to the stove for the purpose of cleaning such accidents.

As I was digesting the information stated on the news, I dejectedly began shaking the dark hair on my head and put my two olive-coloured hands to my face. *I can't take it anymore,* I said to myself. *Nothing makes sense; nothing is real!* I exclaimed aloud for greater impact. I knew no one was physically there with me to listen, but I was.

Unconsciously I re-seated myself on the stool in front of the window and began to think. The only real thing I could ascertain was the warmth of the sun touching my face and the sound of the birds chirping in the trees; everything else was a mockery of its former self. It was like a prolonged practical joke that had spun out of control. It was at this moment that I no longer cared about the soccer match. I knew that it was the day to act. If I didn't, I was sure that I was going to be swept away with all the others into the outer insanity that surrounded me.

Having made the difficult decision to act, I quickly switched off the radio, poured another cup of coffee, and stared out the window into the warm July day. At that point I did not want the aggravating event-filled news to violate my ears. I wanted to concentrate all my attention on carrying out my premeditated plan. I no longer cared about being caught and executed. I just wanted to act.

I needed to be able to break free from the bonds I had shackled to others and myself. Acting was also a chance for me to appear, and speak in public—something that no one had been able to do for nearly two years.

The thought of acting was invigorating. I almost swooned at the thought of being able to start something new, irreversible, and unpredictable that I nearly fell off of my stool into the puddle of coffee slowly streaming down the floor.

Feeling that way, I wondered to myself why I had waited so long to decide to act. In that moment, I also understood for the first time what made people like my old roommate risk everything to salvage the same opportunity for themselves and others.

The more I contemplated the idea, the more excited I got. It was not long before all my thoughts began to run together allowing me to temporarily leave the reality of the empty and desolate surroundings of the Republic and imagine something new. Acting was an opportunity to run up against the inertia and madness that had manifested itself since the fateful event. I knew the outcome of my actions would result in immense pain and, ultimately, death; but at that moment I felt refreshingly free.

Buoyed by the prospect of enacting my previously planned activities, I felt my stomach clench into a large knot that nearly caused me to double over on my way to my cordless telephone that I had carelessly left on the ledge of my iron balcony the night before. I needed the phone to inform my office assistant that I was ill and unable to go to work. Calling to report one's absence was mandatory regardless of one's level or position. Failure to do so resulted in the generation of an automatic arrest warrant and a one way ticket to prison 535.

When I hung up I smiled. It was the first smile I had in a very long time that it almost hurt.

It was liberating not go to work. I had grown to despise my administrative responsibilities and the noise-filled, busy, and utterly voyeuristic cubicle-filled office. Most of all, I detested my daily meetings with the vice chancellor magistrate. He enjoyed hearing the updates of the apprehended terrorists at the border crossings. In some sadistic way, I think he enjoyed me telling him more than hearing about it. It was all in the report. He knew I had become uncomfortable with the policy and administration. He saw me wince and limit eye contact. My behaviour amused him. He enjoyed torment and suffering; inflicting misery made him most happy.

After completing the call, I frenetically began preparing for the day. I washed the dishes in the sink, had a shower, and put on my favourite pair of shorts and top. While doing all these things, I could hardly contain my enthusiasm. I felt like a child stealing a cookie from the cookie jar. I knew what I was about to do was legally wrong, but the potential reward made the awaiting punishment well worth any pain I might endure.

Wandering about my apartment, my mind was whiling. I went over my plan in my head several times so I would not forget anything. This was my only chance, so I had to do it right.

After giving my apartment one last examination, I headed for the elevator. While waiting for the elevator to arrive, I experienced a brief moment of sadness at the realization that this would be the last time I would ever be there. Then the down button rang and the doors opened. I entered the elevator and pressed level 1. As soon as the doors shut, I took a big breath. I knew there was no going back. He would be there waiting for me. In fact, I was certain he was already there, most likely innocently handing out candy to children he passed in the park.

By the time the elevator reached the lobby, the bells encased in the gilded clock tower on top of the old central cathedral rang a slow bombulating twelve. *High noon. The ideal time for a showdown,* I chuckled to myself as I entered the street. I knew it was a cheesy thought, but I felt I had to entertain myself as I walked into the unknown.

The cathedral was one of the original city buildings. It was completed at the time the country had officially become a republic. It was an impressive structure that took hundreds of men and fifty years to build. Besides the modest town hall, built and designed by the same crew and architect, the cathedral became the social gathering spot of the city. It dominated the city surroundings in both size and significance and is inextricably tied to the long history of architectural prominence of the Republic, and the clock tower in the cathedral was the tallest in the world at the time of its construction reaching up to two hundred feet.

For many generations, all the weddings in the community were held in the cathedral. When the town hall burnt down in the great fire that destroyed half of the city, the cathedral also served as the school and the legislature until a new school and town hall could be built.

After the event, the cathedral began to lose its prominence and stature as a spiritual and social meeting place.

The magnitude of the event caused a number of people to begin questioning the efficacy of religion and spiritual power so much so that many of its former congregation stopped attending the weekly services. When the badges were introduced to the entire citizenry, the cathedral became permanently vacant to the local population Except for the hourly ringing of the bells, it only opens its old dark mahogany doors between the strict hours of nine and five to foreign tourists who are seeking a glance back at the greatness of history and perhaps a replicated souvenir of a time long passed.

Although the park was a good fourteen large city blocks away from my residence, and the objects I was carrying were heavy, I decided it was better to walk. The only downside to this decision was the weight and awkwardness of my materials. I had about twenty-five pounds of papers in my backpack, and I was carrying an old wooden apple crate filled with extra literature.

However, regardless of the physical burden on my underdeveloped muscles, it was a beautiful day. The weather was so perfect, and I did not want to ruin my last day in the world on the over expensive, crowded, dirty, and slow public transportation system that was unreliable at the best of time and had the deleterious effect of instantly putting me in a bad mood each time I ventured to step onto the decaying tram.

The walk to the park took me thirty-five minutes. I had never been a fast walker, and the burden on my shoulders caused me to walk even slower. For the most part, it was not so bad, but I did have to stop a few times to readjust my hold on the crate. I missed my bike. I badly wanted to ride it to the park because I feel almost crippled without it, but the crate and papers would have made the ride more awkward and frustrating than having to stop once or twice while walking on the way to the park.

Seeing the park in the distance helped to quicken my pace. I really want to put down the crate and take a rest

As I neared the park, my heart began to race and my stomach clench. Both the anticipation and fear made it difficult for me to breathe making me involuntarily stop in front of the arched entrance.

I knew that this was the point of no return. Carrying the material would result in an automatic arrest regardless whether I decided to re-conger the nerve to commit my planned crime or not. I also knew that there was always the possibility that my hesitation would amuse him, and he would carry on the game until I did finally choose to act, whenever that would be.

I truly hated him. He was the human carnation of a monster. Most, however, did not see this side and regarded him as a hero, patriot, and outstanding citizen.

On any given day he would wander the streets looking for a small gaggle of children and offer them candy he had in his pocket before he stopped each one of them to inspect their badges looking for a flaw and an excuse to arrest and kill one of them for failing to abide by his twisted and arbitrary laws of imposed the Republic.

Thinking about him made me shudder as well as provided me the necessary impetus to continue to walk through the open gate and suffer the fate that awaited me. It was the only way I knew I could live with myself.

The park was established in the early days of the settlement of the Republic.

The first city mayor had donated it to the city as an inauguration gift from her vast private hunting lands provide a large and central space for families, individuals, friends, and visitors to freely interact with one another. She also wanted all of the local residents to have an opportunity to enjoy the various outdoor recreational activities and wildlife that otherwise are not visible or readily available to all families residing in the confines of the city.

Her vision of the park was intimately connected to her belief in the need for residents to have a relationship with nature. She thought that being in touch with nature was a key component to maintaining and strengthening one's knowledge and understanding of liberty. Consequently she planned the city to have the park as it primary focus.

When the park was established, there was nowhere in the city that it could not be seen. She also wanted the park to be a beautiful and enjoyable reprieve from the growing urbanization and industry that was beginning to dot the pristine landscape.

The park has four entrances and divides the major city blocks. I selected the entrance that leads directly into the botanical gardens. On a summer day, one can smell the fragrance from the myriad of flowers from two blocks away. True to the intentions of the landscape architects of their day, it is the fragrance of the flowers that drew me to enter the park via this entrance.

The aromatic and vibrant colors were absolutely intoxicating. The smell emanating from the myriad of flowers acted as a welcome mask over the burnt stench constantly pluming from the crematorium and gave a pleasant start to the proceedings to know that we still do some things right.

I followed the winding path to the herb garden filled with an array of plants for culinary and medicinal purposes. I loved the colours and smell escaping from the herbs. As I child, I used to come down to the park every weekend and read each herb's description to educate myself on the name and different uses of each plant. Out of habit, I bent down and examined the dill that was reaching its stems to the sky. Instinctively I picked some and gnawed on it as I strolled over to the birds of paradise.

The birds of paradise were my favourite flowers. In all my travels, I found these flowers to be the most exotic and colourful plant in the world. From a distance, they actually can be mistaken for a bird spreading its purple wings on a green plant. After admiring these unique flowers for a long spell, I picked up the resting crate and followed the walkway to the rose garden to view the spectacular array of more than 250 different roses. If it weren't for the single-mindedness of my self-imposed task, I would have spent the remainder of the afternoon there.

The path winding thorough the botanical gardens lead to a fork that offers the visitor three options. The first t option is to go straight down to the large river that teams with duck, swans, seagulls, exotic fish, and free-ranging peacocks. In the past, paddleboats, kayaks, and canoes used to be a mainstay of the river community too. Now all the boats are locked in the rusted shed that borders the right side of the river.

The second option veered the visitor to the left leading toward the children's playground and park restaurant. The third option was to go right and head toward the forest and picnic area. When I reached the fork, I opted to go straight toward the river because I was intrigued by an old weather-beaten man sitting alone on a bench feeding the birds a loaf of bread he had brought from home.

As I approached him to look at the imported black swan waiting patiently for some bread beside him, he looked up and smiled at me with a twinkle in his eye. Then, like all the others in the park, he sat with his eyes fixed on the ground.

His smile disconcerted me. I also thought he could be a spy, and I made a mistake taking this route. I knew no one could be trusted. I may have let my guard down too soon.

It had been a year since I had seen anyone smile and I did not know how to react. Realizing he was harmless, I relaxed a little and had time to reflect on the shared moment of a smile as I turned around to head toward the forest.

His smile was contagious because I found myself humming and smiling as I strolled down the winding path that led through the forest that housed over seven hundred different types of trees. The shade from the oak and conifers was also a welcome reprieve from the warm rays of the sun.

As I neared the picnic area, my smile began to fade and turn into a slight grimace. That time, it was I who was attempting not to make any eye contact. Through the corner of my eye, I noticed I was getting some suspicious glances from other wanderers as I ambled along. In my reverie, I had temporarily forgotten that smiles and personal gaiety had become too rare and, therefore, suspicious. The large wooden box filled with papers I was carrying also was not helping to divert attention.

Although I knew that my badge protected me from any unwanted telephone calls to the terrorist hotline, I hastened my pace. I could already feel the sun growing cooler, and I wanted to commit my crime while it was still light so that my activity would gather as large of an audience as possible. I also needed to unburden myself of the crate and knapsack that by then were almost too heavy for me to carry any farther. Thus, when I reached the foot of the wooded area that overlooks the city hall, I was relieved.

I had chosen this spot for my demonstration both for its symbolic significance and its strategic location. It was the space where the constitution of the Republic was signed, and it faced the busiest intersection in the city, which was guaranteed to draw a crowd.

Gratefully, I placed the box on the sun-baked ground, removed the cumbersome backpack from my aching shoulders and surveyed the area. I was not sure how much time I was going to have before the sound of screaming sirens could be heard in the distance and the wave of black-clad troops could be seen running toward the makeshift platform to block and scatter the congregated people to abruptly bring an unwelcome end to my transgression.

I did not look at my watch before I began my premeditated crime mostly because I was not used to wearing a watch. For that reason, I am not sure how long I was permitted to conduct my oration and distribute the literature. It felt like five minutes, but I knew it had to have been longer because when I began, there were only a few scattered people in the vicinity of my selected area; but by the time the units arrived, I was unable to see the pathway leading through the forest.

This is why I did not want to stop. It was the first time such a large audience had gathered to watch and listen before the terrorist-prevention hotline had been activated. The size of the crowd could have been dependent on the anticipation of a grand arrest precipitated by the colour of my badge, but what mattered to me was that people were there to see, hear, and witness an act in a public place. Although not the ultimate ideal, it was a start.

In the end, I knew that the size of the crowd, the time of the call, and the arrival of the tactical units depended entirely upon the will and personal amusement of the vice chancellor magistrate. He would decide when the exhibition was getting too dangerous and to bring it to an end. As long as he was amused, I had time. However, my goal was not to amuse him; I had already done that for too long.

Regardless of my intention, I am certain that all my acts were entertaining to him. It is uncanny how he knew everything, but he did. He made it his business to know everything before it happened. It gave him the aura of omniscience, which only served to lend support to his unchallenged belief that all human actions can be controlled and predictable. Given this, I knew that he would want me to know that he knew I would commit the crime before I did. More than that, he wanted me to know that he knew the exact date and time I would choose to publicly enact my transgression leaving the door open for the all-too-human possibility of surprise. I knew he was wrong; my administrative assistant probably told him I wasn't in, and he knew where to go.

'The chopper is landing,' a voice echoed through a nearby throat mike jerking me out of my reminiscence.

'It's time to remove the pestilence,' he finished.

As soon as he finished this statement I was forced upright by four burly officers and blinded as an unseen fifth officer shoved a black hood over my head blinding me from the strong rays of the sun and trapping the burning gas on my already burning eyes and nose.

PRISON 535

By their nature, prisons are always uncomfortable places No allowable amenities, such as a computer, can change this fact. Being alone makes it worse. I have no one to talk to except the ghosts in the he sad walls. Every minute they probe deep into my haemorrhaging brain and command me to provide them a home and rest.

Humiliated and ashamed, I shudder as the old and weary ghosts point their transparent hands to the computer. They scoff at my shame and show no mercy. *Remember,* they howl as they circle about my head. *I will,* I promise—almost a plea for them to leaves I can write in silence.

They don't leave though. They want to appear in an effort not to be forgotten. They want to remind me in every waking moment that it is my duty to restore their presence and being through the timeless leaves of the pages of a book.

It is a small victory over my forgetfulness. I hear them cry, shout, and scream. However, as anguished and disturbing as the howling sounds are to my ears, the follow silence that follows their temporary departure is more troublesome to me.

Thrrrrrrrrrrrrrrrrrrrrrrrrrrrrrrrrrrrrrrrrrrrr! the chopper blades thundered as the slick lead vehicle neared the ground. Even with the black hood over my head, I could almost feel the trees bend from the unnatural wind generated from the circling chopper units, making me shiver in the warm air. Regardless of the unexpected chill created from the chopper, and my impending captivity, I was able to conjure a faint smile as I imagined the undistributed papers I had brought whirl and fly everywhere throughout the park and downtown streets. It was an extra advantage that I hadn't calculated into my distribution plans that for a brief moment made the burning in my eyes and face seem tolerable.

Counter to the human understanding held by the vice chancellor magistrate, the thing I counted on the most while devising my plan was human curiosity. What I observed over the thirty-two years of my life was that it is very difficult for people to truly mind their own business. This is why the arrests draw such a large crowd.

Consequently, while planning my crime I anticipated that my impromptu speech would draw a significant crowd from the desire to know what was happening. I also expected people to at least read some of the contents of the papers I distributed for the same reason. The unpredictability of the flying papers was an extra bonus that boosted my spirit and satisfaction in my otherwise dark and distressing circumstance. My impromptu smile faded the moment I was picked up and tossed onto the chopper hitting the titanium floor with a thud.

'The park is now sanitized,' a voice crackled over the uniform-attached throat mike.

'You are clear for takeoff,' an unknown officer announced giving the landed chopper a double knock on the side signalling the chopper to swoop into the air knocking me forward and deafening me with the din of its engine.

As I fell, two officers grabbed me from both sides and forced me to my knees. I was then menacingly informed that I had to remain in this position for the duration of the flight. If I did not, I was informed that my disobedience would result in an immediate and painful reprisal from the transport crew.

Having my hands locked behind my back and my legs tightly chained around my ankles coupled with the motion of the high-speed chopper made maintaining the stipulated position extremely difficult. It quickly became more difficult when my circulation began to restrict and I was overwhelmed by the uncomfortable creeeping of pins and needles throughout my upper and lower limbs. As the sensation of paralysis intensified in my limbs, my body began to teeter precariously back and forth until the chopper veered abruptly to the right causing me to fall forward and hit my head on the outstretched steel-toed boot of the officer stationed adjacent from me.

The result of my falling caused the entire crew to erupt into protracted laughter.

'Get up, vermin!' yelled the officer I hit as he used his hard boot to push my head and body back into its designated kneeling position. 'You scuffed my boot,' he echoed as he punched my head causing me to fall backward and bang my head on the solid side paneling.

'You have thirty seconds to get up or we will all shoot you,' he ordered as he used his boot to put the full weight of his body onto my chest so hard I thought I could feel a rib crack. As he uttered the word *shoot*, the sound of eight handguns cocking reverberated through the chopper's interior.

The last hit from the enraged officer caused a trickle of warm blood to stream from my nose into my open mouth. Every part of my body was throbbing. I did not want to be shot. I knew they wouldn't kill me because that duty was reserved for the hooded executioner after the interrogation. However, the legislation permitted them to use whatever force they deemed necessary to contain me.

Groaning and grasping for air, I began to summon all my willpower to propel my body forward. It was just two feet. Not very far, I coaxed myself. My first attempt failed and I fell further backwards. My failure resulted in another eruption of laughter from the expectant crew.

'Come on, louse,' came a voice from the cockpit.

'You have ten seconds until you will receive a bullet shower.'

Taking his statement as a prompt, the remaining officers began counting down from ten. At five, I was shaking and began to brace myself for the impact. *I would be lucky if I retained my torso,* I thought as I gave one last upward thrust. In my final attempt, I found myself rocking in a slightly upright position. Fighting to maintain my balance in the few seconds that remained, I managed to accomplish the Herculean feat and reinstate the required travelling position on my knees.

'Too bad.' I heard one of them grumble.

'I haven't maimed a rat in a while.'

'No worries, mate,' another responded. 'There is still plenty of time. We are just getting started.'

He then refocused his attention on me.

'Sit tight, little monkey; there will be no more warnings.'

He spat, gave me a small shove with his gruff hands, and began a banal conversation with his partner. Unfortunately for me, at the end of the debacle, the only relief I felt from my achievement was running down my leg and forming a slippery, wet, warm pool under my exposed and folded legs.

During the flight, I was entirely at their mercy; and although the episode felt like an eternity, the last officer's remarks were only too true—it was just the beginning. There was indeed still a long way to travel with the trigger-happy elite tactical sanitation unit officers.

The Department of Internal Republic National Security was inundated with job applications when it issued its first recruitment ad for the sanitation units at the behest of my policy group. The advertising strategy was developed to play a dual role. First and foremost, it was to recruit highly trainable and willing candidates for the new unit. Second, and almost equally as important to the advertising process, was the indirect message of power, safety, authority, freedom, and stability that the creation and implementation of the new unit would bring to the besieged Republic.

The aired and poster recruitment ads colourfully portrayed the sanitation unit as a key part of the Republic's security strategy to promote stability and authority in the growing crisis. The unit was charged with the responsibility to shape the national security environment, assure access to regions of vital interest, and permit timely and effective crisis response from the any part of the Republic.

The ads further specified that the unit was to play an integral role facilitating peace and mitigating internal conflict through its ability to be rapidly deployed to the specified scene of transgression—either visibly, over the horizon, or under the seas. The ads also emphasized that the successful recruits would be trained using the most modern technology and become proficient in the use of sophisticated tactical weapons, sensors, and information systems.

The duties and responsibilities of the sanitary units were simple. They were to respond to calls for service, confront and resolve emergency situations in a manner that protected the Republic, maintain public order, actively respond to problems in the community, enforce laws, and arrest terrorist and criminal offenders.

In the wake of the terrorist crisis generated from the two catastrophic events, the Department of Internal Republic Security Sanitation Unit recruitment campaign reached an eager and receptive market. In only a month, it had received five thousand applications causing a significant imbalance between the number of available positions and the number of applicants. At its three-month window, the department had received over ten thousand applications. Thus, in order to narrow the numbers and recruit the candidates that would most successfully conduct the tasks assigned to the unit, I devised measures to tighten the qualification procedures.

The first set of qualifications each recruit had to pass was the physical exam. In this test, the applicant was required to run four hundred meters on a one-thousand-meter track while wearing a thirty-pound soft weight belt as quickly as possible. At each one-hundred-meter interval, the recruit was ordered to climb up and down a set of twenty steep stairs before continuing the circuit.

At the end of the one thousand meters, the applicant was instructed to sprint twenty meters and clear a four-foot fence. If any part of the recruit touched the fence, the recruit was immediately disqualified from the process. Following completion of the circuit, the participant was ordered to drag a 150-pound dummy twenty-five meters non-stop in twenty-five seconds or less. Failure to complete the task in the allotted time also resulted in immediate dismissal.

The candidates that passed the physical test were given a written exam that was designed to assess their ability to apply basic arithmetic operations such as addition, subtraction, multiplication, division, and fractions. They were also expected to solve word problems such as determining rates of speed and stopping distance.

Each candidate was given one hour to complete fifty questions. Two points were deducted for each unanswered question. The second portion of the written test evaluated the applicant's ability to organize and process orders in a clear, coherent, and direct manner. This test was also scheduled to last an hour. While grading the test, any candidate that expressed a penchant for independent thought was immediately screened out at this stage.

The last test administered to determine the successful recruits was the behavioural personnel assessment test. In this test, the applicants were given two hours to answer a series of personality and psychological questions. The test was devised to isolate the candidates showing the greatest proclivity for sociopathic behaviour.

The purpose of this test was to separate the sociopaths from the rest of the remaining candidates. All applicants outside of the proscribed categories of pathological personality were dismissed. The remaining candidates—the identified glib, manipulative, shallow, lack emotional attachment, craved power, and enjoyed inflicting pain on other without guilt—were hired and sent for training in an undisclosed location in the mountain region of the Republic. These were the people I was flying with. Unfortunately for me, the ones waiting on the ground were a lot worse.

'Are you ready to have some fun?' the pilot jokingly asked the unit crew.

Without waiting for a response, the pilot began to weave the chopper up and down in the hopes that my teetering weary body would once again fall over to provoke an abusive reprisal.

Throughout the journey, I occupied myself by repeatedly counting to ten. It was simple and short enough to keep my attention, but it did make me feel a little insane. However, the perpetual repetition of the numbers gave me something to concentrate on and act as a diversion to the discomfort I felt in my keeling body. As the chopper began undulating at the pilot's behest, my concentration broke at seven. It took every ounce of muscle control to stop my body from falling forward onto the cold metal floor.

Not having achieved the desired goal, the pilot quickly revised his flight plan to include a series of high-speed 360-degree turns. There was nothing I could do. Gravity and fatigue prevailed. As the chopper swung sharply into its spin, my knees buckled, and I slammed sideways onto the floor leaving my unprotected body exposed to my bloody fate.

When I hit the floor, the unit erupted into a crescendo of applause followed by the metallic click of a single handgun opening its mouth for fire. The heavy hood on my head negated the need to close my eyes to hide the impact of the impending blast from the cocked firearm, but I did anyway.

'Now you can take your target practice,' the co-pilot yelled over his shoulder.

Without hesitation or a verbal reply to the invitation, the bored officer released his waiting bullet from the nozzle, which whizzed straight into the heel of my left foot.

The hit sent me tumbling backward into the side of the chopper. The pain in my ankle was so intense that my scream of agony was muted. In my head it was a sonic boom, but my mouth and lungs were unable to produce the desired response. Instead I did my best to use the wall of the chopper as a prop to steady myself into the required kneeling position and change my thoughts from the steady flow of blood streaming from my left ankle.

'Nice shot, mate.' I heard as the back of my neck was being grabbed forcing me back onto my knees.

'That will teach you to do what you are told,' he continued.

'Our orders are to get you to prison 535 alive, but there is nothing in our instructions that it has to be in one piece,' he sneered.

'The next fall will result in a hole for your other foot or, better yet, the loss of your leg.'

The sound of the prison name nearly evaporated all my resolve. It was a good three-hour flight, and we had only been airborne for half of that. I would have to think of something more stimulating than counting to ten if I had any hope of making it through the rest of the journey unscathed.

Prison 535 opened its doors six months into my tenure as the director of the Department of Internal Republic Security. Opening the prison had become essential to house the growing number of convicted terrorists in the Republic that were beginning to overpopulate the scattered prisoners around the Republic. Prison 535 also had the added logistical advantage of being a previously built facility with plenty of cells and interrogation rooms located in the middle of the arid desert making it the ideal place for insurgents to disappear and no longer be a threat to the safety of the Republic.

Before being transformed into a penitentiary, the 535 facility was the home of an infamous psychiatric institution built to cure the mentally insane nearly a century ago. The institution was administered by an experimental group of doctors who believed that mental illness could be cured through torture.

The idea behind the institution was to remove diagnosed mentally ill patients from society and force the illness out of the body. Consequently, the facility was built in the middle of the desert and resembled more of a prison than a hospital. The prison inherited its name from the number of patients that were killed from repeated physical torture at the hands of the doctors who were entrusted to protect and provide support to their illness.

The experiments conducted at the hospital ranged from sleep deprivation to surgery, intimidation, coercion, shock therapy, drug-induced stupors, ice-water immersion, bloodletting, lobotomy, straightjackets, and lockdowns. And when the doctors discovered that the treatments were ineffective and, in most cases, worsened the manifestation of the mental illness in the patients, they made a collective decision to sterilize the patients believing it to be the only way to contain the spread of mental disease.

Shortly after the sterilization process had begun, the experiments conducted at the institution were discovered and exposed by a freelance journalist doing a piece on the effectiveness of the new techniques. The administrator attempted to have the journalist committed and lobotomized to keep the information about the centre secret but was befriended by an attendant who helped the journalist escape. Upon his return to the capital, the investigative journalist wrote a critical article that exposed the horrific conditions and practices carried out at the isolated centre and the exploits of the administrator to avoid exposure that fuelled a nationwide public outcry to close the psychiatric institution.

Responding to the wave of protests, the administration sent in select military personnel to arrest all the doctors, workers, and administrative staff involved in the treatment practices and stopped the transportation of new patients to the experimental facility. The administration also purchased the building and locked its doors to the dark ghosts until the new terrorist edict drafted by my department two years ago.

Over the past two years, it has become common knowledge that those who enter 535's large barbed steel gate suffer the worst forms of torture and execution. This I knew very well. I read and signed all the reports. While I was riding in the chopper, my spirit wavered at the thought of entering the fortress that had become the Republic's most notorious security symbol ran by the most diabolical prison staff.

The guards at 535 are all former criminals convicted of multiple murders, rape, and serial killings. They were released and recruited to 535 by the Department of Internal Republic Security as a means of freeing space in the overcrowded penitentiaries and giving inexpensive freedom for them to conduct their twisted fantasies while at the same time keeping them housed in a safe, secluded prison environment.

I stared fixedly through the small oval window pondering my arrival. The chopper had just passed the ring of snow-capped mountain that hemmed in the vast wind-rippled desert that signalled the end of the journey. The empty dry desert stretched ahead of us in great rolling plains. From high above the sand dune plains, it looked such a dry, waterless, wretched place that was not designed for human habitation. *It was the perfect place to die,* I thought as we sped past a cavern that contained a mass of unmarked grave of decayed animals' bones that had obviously died a slow-lingering death in the silent, lonely desert.

When the sun disappeared into the pink horizon, there was nothing but a suffocating darkness. The only light illuminating the solitary wasteland was the beam from the moving chopper. For an instant, we were engulfed in complete darkness as a dense swirl of soft brown sand generated by the rotating chopper blades curtained the chopper. Straining my eyes through the thick granulated sand, I caught an unwanted glimpse at the grey and barbed-wired walls of what soon would be my new home.

I was freezing. The shorts and T-shirt I had opted to wear that morning were offering me no protection from the chilled desert air. My body was shivering, and the metal from the heavy steel shackles squeezing my wrists and ankles constricted serving to intensify the cold running through my body from the dark desert night.

Suddenly the chopper slowed and began to lower itself down to the yellow-white stream emanating from the guard tower that dominated the vacant sandy courtyard and guided the chopper to its landing dock inside the thick stonewalled prison. Nearing the ground I was able to distinguish the mass of black objects as the gang of prison guards who were uniformly swinging their nightsticks in anticipation of my landing. I was not looking forward to their greeting.

As I was contemplating my reception, the chopper motionlessly landed on the asphalt pad. My whole body was shivering, and I wasn't sure I was going to be able to move. During the flight, my body had stiffened firmly into the kneeling position from the cold making it nearly impossible to move. Unfortunately for me, that was not an option.

'Out you get, louse; the ride is over,' an officer urged with a solid kick to my cracked rib.

I doubled over in agony and lay immobile on the chopper floor. My immobility angered the crew who were eager to return home. In response to my uncontrollable defiance, I received another kick to the rib and felt a large hand grip the back of my shirt pulling me upright.

Once on my feet, I almost fell back over. I could barely stand. Both my legs were asleep, and my ankle was still bleeding from the bullet it received earlier. In the grasp of the impatient officer, I remained still for a moment in a genuine effort to gain a sense of balance. Not wanting any more external prompting, I regained my composure and began to slowly hobble forward until I felt air. I missed the step and tumbled hard to the granular ground, which rendered me unconscious for an undetermined length of time.

When I awoke, I discovered that I was encased in a shade less yard, shackled, stripped naked, and exposed to the blazing heat of the sun. The only company around me were a tall white guard tower, a twenty-five-foot metal-chain-linked and top-spiked fence, and the big yellow burning sun that had succeeded in heating the metal to a point that branded my unprotected flesh.

In an attempt to liberate myself from my circumstances, I tried to move my body toward the small shadow created by the guard tower. From where I was lying, it seemed like a veritable oasis. In vain I tried to nudge my body forward. The chains on my legs were too tight, and my head was pounding.

While I was summing the energy for another attempt, I felt my body being instantly relieved from the draining heat of the sun with no effort required on my behalf at all. The shade felt so good that I almost wept. Without hesitation, I directed my eyes into the glaring light of the sky only to discover the source of the miracle. A tidal wave of white-yellow sand was rolling across the open desert gaining momentum on its way to the open prison courtyard where I lay lame, defenceless, and completely exposed.

Shortly afterward, the sun had disappeared and all I could hear was the deafening howl and roar of the wind as it carried thousands of unrestrained particles of sand toward me. Less than a minute later, I was struck by a furious blast of wind that engulfed me in a sea of dust and sand that blanketed my skin. I soon began to choke as the eddy of sand entered my exposed mouth, eyes, nose, and ears.

Small rocks unrelentingly pelted my helpless body and continuously flew around me as the dark wall of whirling sand that virtually turned day into night. Hours later, the sun reappeared in full force bringing with it a hot wind that continued to blow across the desert until dusk when my body broke out in cold sweat from dehydration and heatstroke.

I lay on the ice-cold ground in a huddled position in a futile attempt to warm my sun-scorched, cracked, parched, and burnt body. After what felt like an eternity, I was approached by three guards who strutted up to me carrying their poised automatic rifles and asked in a concerned tone whether I was thirsty or not. Not knowing the reaction, I eagerly nodded in assent.

'Great,' the guards responded, 'because we have lots of liquid for you.'

Within seconds of their arrival, one of the guards grabbed my clenched mouth to hold it open while the other two lowered their pants and proceeded to urinate all over my face and into my mouth. 'I bet you are still thirsty, louse,' the one holding my face said as he stood up and relieved the contents of his full bladder onto me while the others urged him on.

'Always refreshing until the last drop,' he said zipping up his dark blue pants.

'We wouldn't want you to die of thirst,' he scoffed cueing the other guards to erupt in laughter.

Immediately following the humiliating episode, I was bombarded with a rain of spit causing me to wretch, gag, and vomit.

My reaction only encouraged them to produce a larger volume of spittle to spray over my prostrate body. When their mouths ran dry, I was hauled up and forced to walk through the large cast iron gate leading into a large barren concrete room at the end of the yard for processing.

The room contained a row of open showers, an old wooden desk, and chair with straps and electrodes attached to it. On the desk was a glass of water, some bread, cheese, and a camera.

'It's too bad the warden isn't here,' another guard sneered.

'I guess we will have to take care of you until he returns.'

'He wouldn't want you to soil his furniture with your filthy body,' another guard replied, 'so you will have to shower.'

After completing the pronouncement, the guards steered me toward the shower stalls where they pulled out a long rubber hose and began blasting me with ice-cold water. The power of the spray was so strong that it knocked me of my feet and slammed me backward into the concrete wall. The force of the artic spray then caused me to slid down the wall and hit my already-concussed head against the water faucet. When I looked down, I could see a tinge of red begin to add color to the mud pool below my feet that I was quickly sliding toward.

'Careful, maggot, you will get yourself all dirty again; stand up so we can finish cleaning you up,' a short rotund guard said holding a small white towel to dry me with.

Fighting the force of the water bursting from the hose, I managed to slowly slide myself upright along the wall. When I was upright, the hose was turned off, and the officer holding the towel stepped forward to dry my dripping and hypothermic blue body. 'You need to look pretty for the pictures,' he said lasciviously rubbing the towel down my back. 'You are a fine specimen,' he continued as he moved the towel up and down my chained legs.

'We are going to have lots of fun with you,' he finished, smiling and placing the towel onto the desk.

'It's your turn,' he indicated to an officer holding a camera.

'Say cheese,' he said as a blinding flash hit my eyes causing me to see square white cubes everywhere I looked.

I shut my eyes, but the glowing images remained. He took a barrage of pictures of every part of my body, only stopping to adjust my position. The last shot I remember was the anal probe. 'It is for our documentation,' he said as the guards madly exercised their male authority in a circle around me.

When the snapping stopped, I was grabbed, pulled, shoved, and strapped into the large wooden chair that had a black extension cord leading to the socket in the grey wall. I vigorously shifted my head from side to side to prevent the electrode helmet from being attached to my head but lost the battle rather easily to the two burly guards who constrained my head.

Knowing I lost the battle, I did my utmost to brace myself for the series of electric shocks that soon would reverberate through and char my already-burnt body using the metal chains still secured around my wrists and ankles as an electrical conductor. I shuddered. The attack arrived, and I was bombarded with a pulse of electric shocks that entered through the electrodes clamped to my head frying me from the inside out. The last thing I remember before losing consciousness was my body convulsing in an electrically induced seizure.

When I came to and managed to open my bloodshot eyes from my pounding head, I saw a pale thin man wearing a pin-striped black suit sorting a pile of papers on the desk. He looked to be in his mid-forties with wavy brown hair and piercing blue eyes. From the way he shuffled the papers and sat hunched at the desk, he closely resembled the thousand of other bureaucrats who show no allegiance to a cause but thrive on getting ahead by following orders and executing suspected terrorists without a second thought.

'Oh, you're awake,' he politely said officiously looking down on my slumped charcoal-colored body.

'I can now properly process you. I already have your DNA sequence number,' he said looking down at a piece of paper on his desk.

'And I see here that you have been cleaned and photographed; all I have left to do is to stamp the charges against you and give your prison uniform so you can be on your way to your cell.'

'Let's see,' he said rather mundanely as he picked up the paper from the desk.

'You are charged with the capital offence of participating as a leader, organizer, and instigator in the formation and execution of a conspiracy to commit a subversive plan against the Republic. You are also charged with the capital offence of waging a war of aggression, disrupting the civilian population and violating the peace and security of the Republic,' he closed absently placing the paper back on the paper-strewn desk.

Lying twisted and contorted on the ice-cold concrete floor where the guards had deposited me, I just stared blankly at the warden as he was speaking. I did not hear much of what he said. I was too worn-out, and I really did not like him and want to give him the satisfaction of an uneventful processing and execution.

I did not want him to know that I had had some serious thoughts of suicide since my arrest, and I most certainly did not want him to know how much at the time of the electrocution I had genuinely wanted to die and have the mounting misery end. This knowledge would give him too much pleasure, and there was no way I was going to contribute to that feeling. I knew he probably thought this was going to be an easy and routine case for him and that he was eagerly anticipating the opportunity my death would be for his career both personally and professionally.

I had no real notion of what horrors were in store for me down the stairs at 535, but at the time and now, the thought of how my defiance would stifle his ambitions helped motivate me to endure the ensuring ordeal. I despised him, and he despised me.

The warden was one of those efficient, fawning people who would follow orders without a question. He also had an annoying penchant for spouting endless clichés, flattery, and basic conversational drivel whenever he spoke. His sole objective in life was to please his superiors and obtain a functionary promotion. He possessed absolutely no personal values of his own and was easily silenced in a verbal debate, mainly for his lack of independent thought.

In every way, he was the ideal candidate to be the warden for 535. It is why he was able to climb his way through the government ranks after graduating from the academy. The top professors and government officials knew that and encouraged him to progress through the bureaucratic examination process. As obvious as his predilection for sycophancy, was his more predominant eagerness to betray a friend, colleague, or a family member just to move up the bureaucratic ladder was his greatest assest.

With him as the warden I knew I was in for the most trying physical test of my life. During the time I lay charred, naked, fried, and burnt on the concrete prison processing floor, the uncontrollable gleam in his steel blue eyes gave away his immense joy that he experienced from my debasement. Everything he had worked for over the last few years was suddenly within his grasp.

On top of that, my arrest and incarceration at his prison presented an excellent opportunity for revenge that he planned to savour as icing on his career advancement cake. He thought that he, and not I, controlled the timing of my death. *What a prick,* I thought to myself. However, I kept my composure and did not speak in order to facilitate the faster closing of his rambling that would culminate in the delivery of the bright orange jumpsuit that was to cover my naked skin.

I had not trained him. He had progressed through the academy on his own. He had obsequiously been climbing his way through the correctional bureaucracy to become the warden of prison 535—the pinnacle of his shallow career.

I had met the warden several times before my incarceration at government functions. At each of these occasions he continually attempted to garner my approval in a vain effort to join my policy division. At each approach, I made every effort to close the conversation and move away from him.

I could see that my repeated spurns greatly aggravated him, but I had never been open to obsequious behaviour. It is a trait that bothered my colleagues, but my position and abilities gave me a degree of immunity to the internal bureaucratic manoeuvrings. Despite this, his desperation for career advancement and recognition kept him pursuing my attention, recognition, and approval.

No amount of social shunning could relieve his presence from my own. And there I lay on his floor at his prison to be killed at his instruction. Ironic, but there are always people that one cannot escape, the most important one being oneself.

From my contorted and blurred position on the floor, I could still discern the sinister gleam in his eyes as he processed the litany of forms for the Republic's official records. In the past year, the number of arrests had slightly declined, which raised the possibility of closing the costly prison.

The reason for the considered closure was simple. The sanitation plan had been extremely successful—more successful than the chancellor magistrate and hand-selected legislature could have imagined. As the primary architect of the policy, I was sickened by its success. The warden, on the other hand, was ecstatic. He had made several appeals to maintain the institution and increase the social vigilance required to capture more terrorists. Now that I was one of them, he could barely contain his excitement.

He finally finished speaking and summoned the guards to escort me to my cell. When they arrived, I tried to stand up on my own accord but was unable to do so. I was still suffering from post-shock tremors, and my eyesight was blurred. In this state I was incapable of either walking or clothing myself, so a group of four guards had to come and lift me up and force me into the orange jumpsuit held by the bemused warden.

When this was done, two guards grabbed me by each arm and proceeded to drag me listlessly down the long row of empty steel cages equipped with small double-barred windows toward the dark shadow at the end of the hall. In the empty hallway, each step from the guards' black steel-toed boots produced an eerie echo throughout the vacant cell house.

When we arrived at the end of the cell-lined hall, I saw a long slippery dark stone staircase that appeared to lead down into the depths of oblivion. On my naked feet, the stairs felt damp and cold. They were worn, uneven and curved into a dark alley with a faint light in the distance.

Reaching the light offered no comfort. It illumed a large open chamber filled with various sadistic devices resembling medieval torture instruments used for eliciting confessions or inflicting punishments on transgressors. In this case, they were the rusted old instruments for curing insanity.

Then a voice barked, 'Face the wall! Hands behind your back!'

In my horrified and shame-induced stupor generated from the sight of the instruments used to dismember so many previous residents, I hadn't noticed the small wooden door located to the left beside me.

I could not believe I had been so negligently callous to sanction the reopening of such an institution. It was at that moment that I realized how pathetic and cowardly my previous career ambition had been. Thousands before me had been cruelly tortured and maimed to death before being ruthlessly shot in the back of the head in the cell I was about to enter. It was now my turn.

Pushing aside the rush of thoughts, I complied with the order and turned my head toward the awaiting door. I did not have to worry about my hands because the two guards escorting me had already pinned them tightly behind my back.

There was no window on the door, only a small sliding slot that can be opened from the outside to insert small portions of food that is never used and rusted shut. This did not matter as I wasn't expecting food or at least I did not want any that they would select to feed me.

The cell resembled a hole more than a room. The thick windowless walls and floor were made from black slate rock that had the effect of making the cell appear even smaller than its diminutive dimensions. The black walls and earthen floor combined to create a damp and claustrophobic atmosphere. In place of a toilet, there was a large hole in the floor with an odour so repugnant my stomach was constantly battling the urge to wretch and vomit. Also embedded in the earthen floor was a metal chain anchor located diagonally in the floor from a metal bar that was extended across the black stone ceiling.

Having barely an opportunity to survey my new residence, I was handcuffed to the metal bar in a fashion that prevented my feet from touching the ground. When my arms were secured, another guard chained my feet to the protruding metal hook in the floor. After securing my limbs, a rope was attached to the handcuffs and hung around the bar to create a pulley that was used to the stretch my limp body to hang in an uncomfortable lifeless manner in the damp, dark, and unventilated hole.

Each day I was subjected to a new form of physical and psychological torture. This was done to both humiliate and encourage me to accept my death sentence with the least amount of resistance—something that I was determined not to do. However, regardless of my intentions, the sound of the guards' boots echoing in the vacant hall and the placing of the old key into the iron lock to announce the arrival of my next round of torture struck fear deep into my soul.

On the first visit to the torture chamber, I was whipped then bound in a straitjacket for hours until my face, hands, and neck would become numb. Eventually, my limbs turned black from a lack of circulation, and I passed out. The next trip left permanent damage to my already-injured body.

On that occasion, I was tied to a rack and stretched gradually for an hour, which abnormally elongated my body. During the painful process, I could hear my joints systematically dislocating at each loud popping sounds that make me wince in agony. While I was tied to this horrible devise, a guard would then employ a variety of more subtle tortures. I was burned with red-hot pincers and whipped with a rusted chain until my body was covered in welts of blood.

The following day, the torturer entered with his assistants and tied my hands behind my back. Then a guard raised me up by means of a pulley attached to the roof of the chamber, which was about fourteen feet high. After I had been hung there for about an hour, the rope was released suddenly.

The release brought little relief to my aching body. As soon as I was on the ground, a guard tied a heavy stone to my feet and raised me back up using the pulley. While I was being re-elevated, two other guards pushed over a contraption that resembled an old wooden beer barrel. It was large, brimmed, and open at the top; but I could not see what was inside the container.

Once I was raised again, I was kept there for a while and then dropped into the awaiting wooden contraption. When this occurred, I had an opportunity to discover what was in the barrel. Descending into the barrel, my exposed legs were poked with reeds as sharp as swords. Again and again, I was hauled up until, on the thirteenth elevation, the rope broke; and I fell from the great height into the barrel and was rendered unconscious from the force of the drop.

On another occasion, I was stripped naked and placed in a bath of scolding hot water until it became lukewarm. Afterward I was transferred to another container filled with ice-cold water. During both the hot- and cold-water torture, my nostrils were pinched shut, and vinegar was forced down my throat. After the cold water began to warm, I was removed and hoisted up in chains to hang for the night that allowed the cold desert air to freeze the water on my previously charred and electrocuted skin.

The policy behind prison 535 was to subject each prisoner to a round of increasingly painful punishments as a means of breaking the will to live of the convicted terrorist prior to the interrogation. To accomplish this policy objective, the entire prison staff and administration were given carte blanche authority to use whatever devices and methods deemed necessary to persuade the prisoner to elect to die. When the prisoner cries out in pain, or begged to die, the pain and torture routines were intensified.

It was only when the prisoner becomes the embodiment of death does the true death come. It is a game to the warden. He enjoys seeing the value of life slowly drain away from the prisoners' face until they ostensibly become living corpses. His credo is that as long as there is pain, there is life. It is life that the warden wants to eliminate. However, he wants the prisoner to choose death and to become a corpse—listless, submissive, and completely removed from life. It is only when the prisoner reaches this state of oblivion does the warden scuttle down the hall and stairs, away from the comfort of his office and television monitors to present the hollow opportunity for the interrogation to the lifeless and mutilated prisoner.

When a new prisoner is placed in the windowless earthen cell in the bowels of 535, the warden takes a seat in his comfortable custom-built leather swivel chair dominating his spacious office. In that posture, he ponderously and gleefully rolls from one end of the office to the other never taking his beady eyes away from the wall-to-wall, large-screen color television monitors that display the prisoner in the cell and in the torture chamber. From his chair, he watches every movement and hears every word that the prisoner makes in the eager anticipation of seeing the prisoner mentally collapse into a hanging corpse.

Sometimes the process takes several days while others are over after the first session in the former asylum mental illness recovery room

To be fully prepared for the proceedings, the warden had the department of internal security install a refrigerator, couch, full kitchen, and open washroom in his office. This was done after he had gone to the bathroom and missed the transformation of the prisoner. The event haunted him for several months, and I don't think he ever recovered from the experience and has, henceforth, made arrangements to have every amenity built into his office so he is never in the position of missing the psychological death of another prisoner.

For one particularly stubborn prisoner, he documented in his reports that he had to sit for two straight days and nights without eating or drinking, anxiously looking for signs that indicate the imminent mental and physical collapse from the prisoner. When the signs appeared, the warden noted that he was able to relax. He had felt his eyes begin to twitch and involuntarily close and was concerned that he might miss what he described as the grand finale.

Feeling so relieved, he continued his report; he poured himself a glass of a twenty-year-old imported scotch with no ice, opened some caviar, sliced some baguette, and had a small picnic while he patiently awaited the last drop of life to drift from the prisoner's eyes on the multiple row of large-screen television monitors. 'After I ordered the guard to shoot the prisoner,' he concluded, 'I slept like a baby.'

The moment the warden witnessed the last bit of resistance and hope and life drift from the afflicted prisoner's face and body, he presses the guard alarm to summon the frolicking guards to the prisoner's cell. When the guards hear the constant ring of the alarm, they reportedly enthusiastically stop their leisure activities, dress themselves in their government-issued uniforms and combat boots, grab their flashlights, and load their handguns. Once ready, the designated captain contacts the warden using the intercom installed in the guard quarters. The warden then joins the waiting guards to lead him down the empty cell-lined hall to the concrete stairwell where they storm the hole where the forlorn prisoner hangs abject and emotionless. The warden then returns to his office to watch the proceedings from the comfort of his easy chair.

Since prison 535 opened its doors to prisoners of the Republic, the same outcome has been registered in each of the post-mortem reports. The captain removes the tight shackles from the hands and feet of the suspended prisoner who, incapable of standing, instantly crumbles motionlessly to the floor. While the prisoner is on the floor, a guard calls the warden on the speaker, then leans down, and places the small cell phone to the exposed prisoner's ear. When the phone is position beside the prisoner's ear, the warden who continues to watch the activity of the prisoner on the row of monitors informs the prisoner that it is time for the interrogation.

No prisoner has ever responded to the announcement. Instead, each one has remained inert—no longer capable of responding or willing to have a conversation before taking in the last breath. Regardless of the repeated outcome, each time the warden announces the pending interrogation he lustfully gazes into the streaming monitor, licks his lips, and eagerly rubs his chubby hand before enumerating the two options available to the prisoner.

Subsequent to announcing the arrival of the interrogation, the warden pauses to take in the enjoyment of the proceedings, then states to the prisoner in an overly friendly tone that the interrogation is not necessary to endure. He mentions that that can be avoided if the prisoner wishes to accept immediate death in the putrid cell by a volley of bullets into the body from the handguns of every guard present.

To go to the interrogation, the prisoner has to say interrogation firmly into the microphone. To accept the bullets, the prisoner just has to slightly move a digit or a limb. Since the doors to the illustrious prisoner were opened, every inmate, except for me, has chosen to skip the interrogation. For them, after being deprived the dignity, sustenance, meaning, and freedom as well as being subjected to daily and nightly torture, they did not care to partake in the last human vestige of freedom. They did not want to attempt to summon the useless energy to appear in front of a peer and have an opportunity to explain oneself before dying.

It was easier to accept death mainly because they had already given up on life. I was determined not to do so. It was the only reason I allowed myself to be arrested. It was the only way I could imagine to reinvigorate life, meaning, and freedom.

The interrogation is the reason why I elected to come here. The warden was not going to get his immediate satisfaction, and I was in for a great deal of more pain. It was considered a failure to have to summon the interrogator from the capital. He was a stern man who did not enjoy flying and especially disliked the arid desert air.

The crude, raw, and humiliating daily abuse I received at the prison repeatedly tried my resolved and constitutional threshold. Every day leading up to my interrogation brought upon a new nightmare. The torture techniques previously administered to the mentally ill to exorcise the inner demons only served to reawaken my own. I was always alone and incapable of leaving myself. In this restrained position, I could only exclaim horror at my complicity in the demise of the Republic.

After the silent and demented guards administered the stipulated punishment, they sinisterly disappeared into the darkness leaving me to ponder my haunted thoughts in the greatest amount of physical discomfort. Ironically, the physical pain was no match for the demon in my head that repeatedly gazed into my dejected soul and reminded me of my active and passive role in reopening the mouth of hell that is prison 535.

Each trip back to my cell resulted in me being force-fed with water, urine, and a goulash of unidentifiable food to retain the physical life processes. When my feeding was completed, the attending guards would hoist my limp body into the wrist and leg shackles to once again stretch me and between the ceiling again. Hanging there on the endless days and nights, I meditated on all the topsy-turvy things that turned me onto this fatal path.

Each night after my regime of punishment was over I hung abjectly transfixed staring into the film playing in my head of all the horror and destruction I have helped cause. My previous thoughts of suicide had evaporated like water into the dry desert air. Despite the constant torture, I finally felt free and aware—conscious of myself as a person and an actor.

It was in those lucid moments that I realized that every act I made prior to my journey here had been a slow suicidal spiral into oblivion. That is the strange thing about seeing the end of your life near. I discovered that I had nothing more to lose and a lot more to gain. I have the ability to reflect, contemplate, understand, and become free from the fetters I had invisibly shackled to myself.

THE REPUBLIC

I t is amazing what a difference five years can make.

Everywhere, the buildings look the same; the streets look the same, but yet nothing is the same. It is as if someone flicked a switch and turned everything upside down. The sad thing is, that is exactly what happened. The worse thing is that I am the one responsible for supervising the design of the switch, hiring the electricians, installing the switch, and orchestrating someone to flick it. It was all highly deliberate, efficient, and completely thoughtless.

My parents always told me that the small things are the most important. If I could see them now, I would tell them that I now agree. I would also apologize and request forgiveness for my stubborn instance that the end always justifies the means. Most importantly, I would tell them that I am now ready to listen. If I had listened to them it is highly likely that I would not be lying here in the hot, arid, and sterile cell awaiting my execution. It is even more likely that the philosophical foundation and atmosphere of the Republic would not be so changed.

I miss my parents a lot. I think about them almost every day. I mostly think about my regrets. I was not a good child, and I never expressed gratitude and respect for everything that they did for me. There are so many things that I wish I was able to say to them that I cannot. The time for talking is always in the living. In death it is too late. I am only glad that they died before the tragedy that now defines the Republic occurred. I am even more thankful that they were not alive to see my active role in writing the script.

It grieves me to know how far away from this bright start we have moved. It is almost as if we have dared to repeat the mistakes of the past with a succession of monarchs in our ancestral country that the framers of the Republic attempted to prevent.

The monarchs in our ancestral land had violated the peace and stability of the kingdom by reneging signed treaties with the villagers, suppressing the human dignity, and meting harsh punishments against the defenceless residents of the kingdom. Although the cause and source of our current situation in the Republic is different, the result is the same—mass devastation, fear, military repression, and violation of the signed constitution.

I write here in the full understanding that we are in a historical void. We have no actors or witnesses. And thus we have no past, present, or future. We only have oblivion and anomie. Everything is meaningless and lifeless.

As the events and policies unravelled, I became acutely aware that this was the overriding objective of the vice chancellor magistrate. To accomplish his twisted outcome, he just needed everyone to share his same view, and unfortunately like the children in the story of the pied piper, we hypnotically followed him in oblivion.

Writing the annals of the Republic in the factory of death and enduring the daily regimen of sadistic mutilation and torture meted out eagerly by the resident psychopaths have made me acutely aware of the importance of remembering and documenting history. In my many hours of feverish reflection, I have discovered that being cognizant of one's history allows one to understand where they are now, how they got there, and where they can go in the future.

In a number of ways, history is the most important subject for an individual to study because it allows one to benefit from previous experiences and advance to enable one to improve on previous errors and omissions. In essence, individuals that know and understand history are much closer to understanding the impact of action in the future.

Unfortunately I came to this realization far too late, and the only future I face is death. It is my hope that if by a miracle this tragic historical tract is read by someone other than the angel of death the future can be made different from the society of walking corpses that I have helped create with my pen.

The Republic grew out of a tiny kingdom that was created out of the aftermath of nearly thirty years of anarchy and civil disintegration resulting from a one-hundred-year plague that ravaged and decimated the long-established civilizations on the shared territories almost one thousand years ago. In those thirty years, a number of diverse, ruthless, and vulnerable tribes were formed. None of the self-formed tribes had a stable administrative system or adequate access to resources from which to build shelter or retain food and livestock, making constant raids and attacks from neighbouring warlord's s commonplace.

Eventually, a few militarily strong tribes began to dominate the large landscape that facilitated the creation of loose and aggressive monarchies. The rise of violent monarchs only served to increase the number of attacks and plunder upon the weaker villages. This situation continued for many years after the plague until a young fierce warrior fought and rose to become the monarch of our ancestral land.

Only a few years into his reign the young warrior king was able to establish an invincible army of fearless warriors who frequently fought over territory and, during hard times, occasionally raided—interested in goods rather than bloodshed. However, unlike the other kings in the area, the young warrior king was a good manager. As the king and commander of the vast army, he made it a point to associate with intelligent, just, and skilled advisors that enabled him to become the first king to establish a mobile political on the continent.

In his youth, the king had witnessed many atrocities against his family and friends at the hands of raiding tribes that led him to practice war techniques from morning to night When he was thirteen he was forced to watch a conquering warlord rape, and killed his mother. Afterward, the warlord bound and took him as a prisoner to be sold as a slave to a neighbouring nation for his strength and youth. The night before he was going to be taken to the market to be sold, he managed to grab a sword and kill his guards then escape on horseback to a nearby forest where he took shelter until it was safe to return to his tribe.

For three days the conquering warlord searched for him, but excellent survival skills kept him alive until he could meet up with his scattered tribe. His act of courage against a fierce enemy soon spread his name to all parts of the continent and won him renown and respect as the tribal king despite his young age.

As fierce as he was in battle, he was equally magnanimous in the postwar settlements. Peace was more important to him than pillaging the conquered territories, and it was not long into his reign that he gained the reputation as the mighty diplomat. After conquering a bellicose tribe, he did not burn and destroy all the residents and inhabitants like the other monarchs. Instead, he left the small villages intact and subsumed the land and inhabitants under his dominion. In so doing he was able to simultaneously expand his kingdom and win respect from the neighbouring tribes who were pressing for tribal unification without war.

The process of using military authority to unite the numerous discordant tribes and independent territories continued until the continent was loosely divided into separate nations. His military prowess initially enabled him to add territory to his kingdom, but it was his diplomacy that built the strong and successful sovereign nation.

During his long reign the king spent many years creating a body of law that was to become the rule of the land. The punishments for any legal violation were harsh—immediate death by his sword, but he made known to everyone that he was equally subject to the law himself. Besides codifying a set of rudimentary laws, the king also introduced record keeping and public education. He made himself the supreme officer of the law who was to collect and preserve all judicial decisions, to oversee the trials of all those charged with wrongdoing, and to have the power to issue death sentences creating peace and order throughout his realm.

As his reputation spread throughout the warring kingdoms, many kings began to request meetings with him to discuss the possibility of an alliance and the unification of their kingdoms in exchange for protection and continued control over the territory. In return for their protection, they agreed to pay him an annual stipend.

Preferring peace to war, the king readily agreed to the terms offered and single-handedly forged a vast and wealthy, organized, and civilized central government among disparate and unconnected monarchies.

The agreement made between the former monarchs and the king stipulated that the king had to consult the members of the alliance prior to passing any new laws or engaging in war. This proviso was made to ensure that the king would not attempt to interfere in the regulation of their territories thereby creating the first centralized but weak constitutional monarchy. To be established after the plague.

The king lived well into his old age allowing the flagship kingdom to prosper and firmly entrench the constitutional tradition. When he died, he left all the royal affairs and responsibilities to his only child and son.

From the first day of his birth, the king provided his son the best educators and military and diplomatic advisors that helped him become a competent and respected statesman and military leader. In all battles, he was the first to lead the charge and the last to leave the field. He did not torture, mutilate, maim the defeated kingdoms as their enemies did, or partake in the gruesome displays to elicit fear and discourage potential enemies.

In the kingdom, all the citizens esteemed the prince for his generosity and homage. Every month, he made an effort to visit all the villages in the kingdom to distribute food and money to all persons in need. Thus, when the king died of a stroke at the age of seventy-five, the decorated prince was embraced by the entire populace as the uncontested king of the large, wealthy, and strong kingdom his father had forged from out of a small and vulnerable tribe.

One of the main priorities of the newly crowned king was to establish clear transit routes to all the villages in the kingdom for more efficient trade and military protection. He also commissioned the building of a high stone fortress that surrounded the outer regions of the kingdom to reduce the possibility of a successful invasion.

The infrastructure projects had the added benefit of providing jobs to the less privileged and greatly increased the economic stature of the kingdom making it the largest and wealthiest Kingdom on the continent and earned the yond monarch the reputed title of the Great King by the residents and neighbouring kingdoms alike.

However, while the kingdom had managed to attain a high level of peace and stability under his and his father's reign, one of the neighbouring kingdoms continued to ravage, pillage and destroy a number of smaller principalities in the surrounding local territories of the kingdom. One night the reigning warlord sent in a number if soldiers disguised as peasants who murdered everyone in the village while they were sleeping.

The attack on the village shocked the king. When he heard the news he was purported to have cried before grabbing his cloak and racing from his chamber to ride to the scene of the attack. Seeing the village completely burned and pillaged and all of the bodies of its former residents strewn on the burnt and bloody ground sent him into a rage in which he vowed to find and kill every member in the murderous tribe. Prior to launching the attack the king ordered his men to exchange their weapons for shovels to dig individual graves for all the slaughtered residents. On each grave, he had the soldiers make the approximate gender and age of the deceased victim with the year along with the year and date of the death. After all the murdered people had been buried, the king then hosted a large funeral ceremony where he paid homage to the dead and reiterated his pledge to avenge all the innocent deaths and restore peace and security to the breathed kingdom.

Despite the intentions and military prowess of the kingdom to track down and capture the invaders, it took several months for the king's best soldiers and spies to locate them. They were nomadic warriors who did not stay in any location very long and were familiar with the terrain. They also were able to seek refuge from hostile kingdoms. Consequently, when the king's most elite forces finally found them, they were forced to wait a few months before they could effectively attack them because it was the middle of winter in the mountain region.

The snow and terrain gave the tactical advantage to the invaders who camped out in the caves to hurl arrows and lances on any brave ice climbers. Even when the snows melted and the many trees provided more security to the climbing troops, the king found himself engaged in a long and bloody war that lasted nineteen years and thousands of deaths and a nearly empty royal treasury before the exhausted king could declare victory.

One of the major political flaws monarchies is the issue of monarchical succession. It is now commonly understood that having a hereditary claim to a throne does not necessarily transfer the characteristics of the previous monarch. It is too often the case that while one ruler may be wise, magnanimous, judicious, and use powers moderately, the successor can be selfish and tyrannical and use using the authority of the crown to serve his own ends. Our ancestral kingdom was no exception to this recognized problem.

Similar to his father, the Great King only had one son. This, however, is where the similarity ends. Like many other sons of great men, he was something less than his father. He was a profligate spender of money who burdened his conquered subjects with unpredictable increases in taxes for his insatiable need for money. And torn between duty and detesting it, he drank so heavily that he needed soldiers to invade nearby regions to secure a constant supply of wine for his daily intake.

Since he had taken over the responsibilities of military commander, the majority of the citizens disliked the prince. In all areas of life, the prince displayed poor leadership. He was prone to frequent fits of rage, had a penchant for treachery, had an inexhaustible lust for wealth and power. He also exceeded the bounds of his position and the established law of the land at will.

He also had a reputation throughout the kingdom as a carousing, selfish, greedy, and unstable person who had little interest in the affairs of the state. And, unlike his father, he never made visits to the villages and towns to meet with the village governors to discuss trade and security issues. However he never failed to be present when the taxes were being collected for the treasury. Thus, before his coronation most residents in the kingdom were hoping the king would change the legislation and allow the village governors to select the next monarch.

Some historians say that the king had met with the governors to consider this proposal before he was thrown from his horse breaking his neck after it had been spooked by a loud noise. This speculation can never be validated. The only fact was that the legislation remained unchanged, and his son had become the next king. It is to him that we owe the creation of the Republic.

Within a few months after his coronation, the new king had lost the respect and advice of the governors, crown treasurers, and the general populace for his complete disavowal of the established rules of justice. His administration stopped all consultations with the governors because they disagreed with him and appointed his friends as his advisers whom he quickly transformed into instruments of extortion by granting them full power to preside over the taxing of property, the military, and the royal finances.

On the whole, the advisors were greedy, selfish and petulant men who, much like the king, were preoccupied with drinking and pursuing wealth than attending the political affairs of the kingdom.

The excessive expense on personal luxuries by the king and his advisors created a mini-financial crisis for the administration whose sole goal was to maintain the present level of spending with the least amount of effort. To remedy the crisis, the king and his personal advisors decided to impose a heavy tax.

The new strenuous tax law had an immediate and detrimental effect on the entire population of the kingdom. After the taxes were collected, many citizens found themselves deprived of their savings and unable to make the yearly mandatory payments. The defaults on tax payments had the unanticipated effect of not securing the calculated funds for the treasury. When this situation became more wide-spread the king and his greedy advisors implemented a more ruthless and burdensome tax.

The amended tax legislation mandated a series of harsh and unrelenting penalties for citizens who failed to pay the required tax sums. The punishments included the confiscation of private lands, corporeal punishment, and imprisonment. As well, the responsibility for tax collection was removed from the local governors whom the advisors deemed sympathetic to the residents and given to a newly instituted group of mercenary tax collectors who were paid a percentage of the amount of each collected levy.

The mercenaries were hand selected from the hostile kingdoms and were strategically given a home in each of the villages to monitor the activities of each of the citizens to ensure that they would not attempt to hide any of the owed revenues. Once hired, the edict authorized the mercenaries to capture, harm, and torture any person who attempted to avoid the yearly collection.

Pleasing to the king and his personal entourage of advisors, the newly instituted tax collection method was an instant success. In the first year the royal coffers grew to the prewar levels, and in the second year, the royal treasury was the wealthiest in the continent.

The new found monies enabled the king to re-build and send his army into the surrounding kingdoms to force the less wealthy kingdoms to provide wine and spirits for the guarantee of peace and protection. It did not matter that in the first year alone, the mercenaries were reported to have destroyed, damaged, and burned nearly 25 percent of the residential dwellings and lands in the forty districts that made up the kingdom while collecting the revenues. All that mattered was the 50 percent increases in royal revenues available for him and his advisors to spend on leisure activities.

As the royal coffers grew, the king began to become obsessed with the gathering and possession of money rather than spending the money. One day in a fit of madness he was purported to have ordered his royal guards to murder all his advisors for fear that they would want to spend the collected money on themselves. Following the murders, the king then arranged to have his bed moved into the treasury so he could always be near the money. It was at this time that his insanity and lust for money became uncontrollable.

One night after the king had fallen asleep while counting the number of gold coins stored in the treasury he had a strange dream. In the dream he saw himself standing in a meadow filled with precious jewels and silver. In the centre of the meadow was a running stream made of melted gold that snaked through the meadow as far as he could see. However, while being surrounded by endless wealth, he realized that he was disturbingly alone—he could see and touch endless wealth but could not see or hear any people.

When he awoke, he could not get back to sleep. Despite the pleasure derived from the endless wealth he possessed in the dream, he was deeply disturbed. It strangely had felt more like a nightmare than a good dream. Every time he closed his eyes, he was afraid that he would have the dream again. When he was awake staring at his money in the pale yellow light illumed by the candles, he felt as if he were reliving the eerie part of the dream where he was around massive wealth but all alone. Not being able to sleep, he rushed to the treasury door and woke all the staff agitatedly called for the magician to come and interpret his dream.

The magician was hired by the king to be his nightly entertainer. With the assistance of his daily intake of wine, he had come to believe that his magician possessed strong spiritual powers that gave home the ability to predict the future, read minds, and turn objects into animals. Thus, when he had the dream he could think of no other person to help him than the magician.

Although a great illusionist, the magician did not possess the divine ability to forecast the future or interpret dreams; however, he was very good at being able to listen and understand people and tell them what they would like to hear. Fearing being killed for giving the king the wrong answer, he decided to interpret the dream favourably for the wealth-obsessed and insane king. As a result he told the expectant king that the dream meant that the greatest amounts of riches were within his grasp; all he needed to do was to find a wife to share his wealth with, and he would be happy forever.

Upon hearing the positive interpretation of the dream, the king was elated. He is said to have danced around the treasury singing and throwing coins up into the air. In his jovial spirit, he appointed the magician his top advisor to replace the one he had murdered a few weeks earlier. Unbeknownst to the magician, he was to also be murdered in another fit of envious rage only two weeks later.

The only thing that upset the king about the interpretation was the prospect of getting married. The king had a long history of carousing with many women. In the end, he always found himself dissatisfied. He liked being with women, but he did not relish the idea of commitment. Consequently the idea of marriage was unappealing to him, and he deeply regretted having the dream until the magician mentioned the idea of marrying multiple women, that would allow the king to satiate his lust for multiple partners while adhering to the interpretation of the dream. When he heard this suggestion, he kissed the magician and gave him ten gold coins that he later recovered after his murder.

The only difficulty was his ability to find wives. All the women in the kingdom hated him and he did not want to marry any of his paid partners. Once again, he consulted the advice of his magician who instructed him to use the mercenaries to bring all the beautiful women (married, engaged, or single) to the king for marriage. The moment the suggestion came out of the magician's mouth it was enacted by the king. It was the last advice he was to give.

The mercenaries took on their new responsibilities with great alacrity. They visited every house in the kingdom to examine all the household women to select the finest wives for the king. When a mercenary found a suitable woman to become one of the king's wives, he would bound, gag, and drag her out of the house and test her for himself. When the family, husband, or children resisted they were brutally beaten and sometimes killed and the house torched and burnt to the ground. After burning the property the mercenaries would then arrest the deposed individuals for tax evasion because they did not have any land or money available to pay the required tax.

The kidnappings, burnings, and arrests became so prevalent in the formerly esteemed kingdom that a red glow and grey black cloud could be seen encasing the kingdom from five hundred miles away. The once-free citizens all lived in fear of the mercenary attacks and imprisonment. Many of the women also began to disfigure themselves to avoid the rapes and becoming a member of the king's household, which only encouraged the mercenaries to inflict harsh penalties for resisting the king's law.

Facing continuous harassment, several citizens, with the help of the village governors, travelled to the capital to demand the removal of the mercenary tax collectors, stop the kidnapping of women, lower the tax requirements and release the arrested tax defaulters from prison.

However, before they could reach the castle surroundings the petitioners were ambushed by the King's army.

The resulting battle was short and bloody. The entire band of petitioners were slaughtered and subsequently beheaded by the militant soldiers. The soldiers then collected the decapitated heads and hoisted them on spikes around the castle to serve as a reminder to the royal residents the penalty for questioning the King's will.

The news of the public executions spread quickly throughout the kingdom causing great consternation and complete hatred toward the king from every corner of the vast kingdom. Within days of the executions, the village governors began to hold secret meetings to devise ways to kill the still-childless king and have his more-educated cousin assume the throne. However, shortly before they were to enact their assassination plan, the king died of acute syphilis.

The death of the king was joyously celebrated everywhere in the kingdom. There were village feasts, firecrackers, and festivals. Everyone believed that the new king would rescind his cousin's harsh tax policies, disband the mercenary law enforcers, return the kidnapped wives and women to their families, and restore local administration to the villages. From all appearances, his cousin resembled the Great King. He was charismatic and had a high appreciation of the arts and literature.

However, unknown to the expectant citizens, he also wanted to make his mark in the kingdom by building a bigger and more elaborate castle than his family had built that required significant revenues to build his personally designed palace. The palace was to be huge and lavishly decorated with art from all over the world. It was also to contain a large library and a music room to satisfy his fondness for the arts. For this reason the early jubilation was short-lived.

While the new king returned the women to their families, mostly because he had no use for them, his act of kindness was undermined by his continuation of the mercenary tax enforcers. Worse than his predecessor, the new king consolidated the army to act as a personal force taking all remaining authority away from the governors whom he knew had plotted against his cousin in an attempt to depose him from the crown.

The increasing misery and poverty in the kingdom, the overcrowding of prisons, and the advent of a famine provoked one of the village governors to seek a solution to the unceasing tribulations exerted on his community. One night while ruminating on the problem he suddenly thought of his friend who had become a wealthy merchant in the port kingdom situated on the coast of the continent 800 miles from his kingdom.

His idea was for his friend to arrange work for a large number of destitute village residents on his merchant ships.

Not wanting to wasn't anyone time he decided to leave the next to propose his idea to his wealthy merchant friend.

After riding across the 800 kilometre open prairie the governor arrived in the bustling port city two weeks later. Exhausted, he decided to stop at a local inn located next to the pier where he suspected his friend would be. The inn was conveniently nestled beside the ocean and was the only inn on the continent to serve clients twenty-four hours a day—a welcome reprieve for all weary travellers and sailors.

The tavern itself was cozy and small. At the far corner of the tavern, a wood fire was constantly burning keeping the air warm from the cool ocean breeze that cast a permanent salty chill on the city. When he entered the inn the governor went immediately to the long wooden bar to order a beverage and some morning food.

Because his apparel and features were different from the region he received many strange glances from the merchant clientele. Ordinarily he was not self-conscious, but the constant stares from the crowd made him feel uneasy and anxious to leave.

'Good day, sir. What can I do for you?' the middle aged bar-tender asked in a kind tone.

'I am just seeking some warm food and shelter before I locate my childhood friend.'

'You don't look like you are from around here the innkeeper responded as he poured some beer into a mug and some soup into a bowl.

'Where-a-bouts are you from, he continued as he handed the drink and warm broth to the almost salivating governor?'

'Thank you.'

He took a few sips of the beer and a spoonful of the warm soup and replied pointing eastwards 'I am from a kingdom eight hundred miles from here that is experiencing a famine,'

'Well, sir, there is lots of food and shelter here for you. Tell me, what friend you are looking to find? I know just about everyone in this fair city,' he said, smiling.

'I am looking for the wealthiest merchant,' he replied after swallowing a spoonful of the chowder followed by a long swig of beer.

'Do you know where I can find him?'

'Well there are a number of wealthy merchants in here, he replied waving his hand, but not none of them the wealthiest. The man you seek is not here, but he is easy to find. He is the biggest, loudest, and best-dressed man you will see on the docks.'

Having discovered the location of his friend, the governor gulped down the remaining portions of his food and drink and ran out the door so fast that he almost forgot to pay. Once he reached the dock he used the remainder of his ebbing energy to quicken his pace

Down the narrow cobblestone pier. When he neared the end his dim eyes discerned a group of large men standing in an organized line mechanically removing cargo from three large ships onto waiting carts for transport to the nearby warehouse. It was not until he was almost on top of the men that he spied his now rotund and bearded friend. He was wearing charcoal coloured hose, a bright yellow jacket with a blue tunic and a dark red shirt. *The innkeeper was right,* he thought. *He does stand out.*

When he was within two feet of his friend, the merchant stop bellowing orders to his crew and gave the unwanted intruder a threatening look that made the governor stumble on a raised plank of wood.

'Pardon me, he said, I thought you were . . .

'My friend he shouted, as he embraced the governor with a long and firm bear hug.

'How are you and to what purpose am I owed the pleasure of this surprise visit, he asked?'

'I am fine, the governor replied, but my homeland is not. Things there have gotten so bad that I have taken this long journey to ask you a favour,'

'I have heard rumours. I will of course do what I can. Come sit down, and we will talk over some warm tea,' he said, leading his friend to the tea stand.

'Keep working!' he yelled to his pausing workers who hastily returned to unloading the large crates.

After getting himself and his friend a tea, he returned to their previous conversation. 'Tell me, my friend, what favour can I do for you after you have travelled so far to visit me?'

'I need you to help me resettle thousands of destitute and imprisoned villagers from my kingdom.' The governor then explained that among the famine, high taxes, and cruel treatment received from the tax collector mercenaries, his kinsmen were in a complete state of physical and emotional despair.

Listening intently to his friend's passionate appeal, the concerned merchant informed him that the famine had also affected his city, but on his travels, he had come across some new and lush lands that appeared to be uninhabited that could become ideal homes for any willing travellers. He added that the land mass was large and surrounded three oceans making it ideal for trade. He told his friend that he had tried to persuade his king to colonize the land, but they did not believe that it was there and did not want to invest the required money for its exploration. Finishing this statement, he told his friend that for a predetermined fee, he would arrange to transport all the villagers who wished to move to the newly discovered and uninhabited land.

The governor thought over the offer for a long moment. He, like the reigning monarch of his friend's homeland, was sceptical about the existence of an unknown and rich land but also trusted his adventurous friend. He then thought about all the ramifications of remaining in the kingdom and the promise of a new opportunity the undiscovered land offered. By the time they had finished their tea, both of the men had made a financial deal to transport the willing villagers to the new land.

When he returned home, the governor requested an audience with the king to discuss the pilgrimage of all willing villagers to the unknown land for any fee the king required. Initially the king flatly refused. He did not like the idea of losing potential revenue as well as authority to what he considered a lowly village governor. However, the governor was persistent and made an offer too great for the king to refuse—he could have all his revenues and vast agricultural lands.

After hearing the final offer, the king paced back and forth in the opulent room while he was pondered the offer. He did need an immediate infusion of money to finish the library in his new palace, and the prisoners were becoming too numerous for the jails to house them all. Still, he was reluctant to subsume his authority to a country leader.

He continued to think until he reached the most beneficial solution for him. He told him that he would only agree to the request if all the prisoners and those who wished to follow him to the neighbouring territory were officially excommunicated from the kingdom.

'If they were ever to return,' he said, 'they would be immediately beheaded.'

The leader accepted the harsh contractual terms without delay, and to show his gratitude and a test of good faith, he had the chest full of jewels delivered immediately to the royal treasury. When the chest arrived, the king had all the tax evaders released and transported to the governor's village where he explained his offer to take them to a new land that was free and full of opportunity for everyone.

It was easier to convince the king than the less greedy villagers that there was a new opportunity for them to prosper and live freely in a new land. Many were apprehensive and none had ever left the landlocked confines of the kingdom. The majority of them believed it was better to stay with what they knew than leave their homes and families to travel to a hypothetical land.

Not one easily discouraged, the governor persisted and continued to enumerate all the advantages of leaving. He stated that his friend was honourable and would never lead anyone into a situation or place that was unsafe. In the end, he was able to convince five hundred residents who wished to escape the ever-present threat of beheading, the growing tax burden, and the famine that was afflicting the already-besieged kingdom.

It was midsummer when the agreement was made to allow the villagers to leave the kingdom. The weather was already humid, and waiting longer would make the eight-hundred-mile journey more arduous. It was also good to leave at once before the fall rains and winter weather came over the unforgiving ocean.

In preparation for the journey, the governor arranged to have travel wagons built to move the food, tools, and meagre possessions. The wagons were large, sturdy with high sides, and had strong broad wheels that made them capable of crossing rutted roads, muddy flats, and the non-roads of the grasslands separating the kingdom and the port territory.

The constructed wagons were also sturdy enough to carry three tons of weight and travel at a moderate speed, thereby reducing the three-week journey into two.

Enough food was packed to last for the entire journey, but because the travellers were all short of money, they had very little with them but the basics for their journey. There were many nights when they were forced to eat the same food—cheese, dried meat, salted pork, biscuits, wheat, and peas.

Two barrels of beer, cooking implements, bedding, clothing, work tools for making furniture, cutting wood and farming, and weaponry were also loaded onto the wagons for hunting and protection from potential invaders. A few families brought some chickens, but they were to be saved until they reached the new land. Besides some dogs, no other animals were brought with them. Some passengers brought cards, games, and writing material to pass the idle time expected on the long journey.

When the settlers arrived in the bustling port city, they were filled with awe and excitement at the first sight of the blue-green ocean. Many of the travellers abandoned the wagons and ran into the refreshing and inviting salt water. The former village governor let them enjoy themselves while he went to meet his friend and sell the horses for travel fees. It was early in the morning, but many people were already out tending the vendors and setting up the market stalls to prepare for the day's sales.

The sky was cloudless and the breeze light, which made it a much better day to begin the long and unknown journey erasing some of the inner doubts he had about leaving the sure land. He trusted his friend but remained a little uncertain. He did not mind going himself, but he felt more responsibility for bringing so many people onto the mysterious and potentially perilous journey. However, he knew his doubts were too late. The commitment had already been made. The only future any of them had was on a boat leading to an uncharted land.

On the way to the wharf, the two friends discussed financial and transportation details. The merchant informed his friend that he would need to procure another ship to accommodate all the unexpected passengers. In total, he said, they required three ships to carry all the passengers and supplies. He also offered to leave one of the ships behind at the end of the journey to act as a transportation vehicle for transoceanic trade or to be used as a navy vessel to ward off any external attacks.

Arriving at the wharf, both men were forced to stop. In their absence, a large crowd had gathered where the villagers had abandoned the horses and wagons to run down into the glittering water. All the townsfolk formed a human wall in their attempt to catch a glimpse of the strangers jumping in the water and running along the pier.

It took almost twenty minutes of pushing for the two friends to manoeuvre their way through the dense growing crowd to arrange the ships and gather the villagers together for the journey. Reaching freedom, the merchant instructed his friend to have everyone gathered by the ships in an hour while he went to get the third ship.

To better facilitate the boarding of the ships the governor gathered the frolicking travellers to the parked wagons and instructed them to gather all their personal supplies out of the wagons and go wait by the tea stand located across from the moored tall ships that were to transport them to their new home. The tea vendor, who was pleased to see so many potential customers, put on five more kettles and baked more biscuits. The delicious aroma emanating from the vendor stand had its desired effect and within an hour he was sold-out of supplies for the day. Just as the last cup of tea was being poured, the merchant returned with the additional ship.

The ship did not resemble the others anchored in the harbour. It was old and looked like it was on its way to the ship graveyard where it was going to be dismantled for its timber rather than sail across the treacherous ocean to an unmapped land. When the potential passengers saw the ship, they were visibly frightened. No one wanted to travel on the third boat, and many began to fight and force the less agile passengers onto the older boat. The jostling and anxiety increased among the travellers when the additional ship was being loaded. The more cargo that was loaded, the lower the ship sunk into the water.

In an effort to quell the fighting and assuage the notable fear on the faces of those forced to travel on the older ship, the merchant stepped between the passengers and assured them all that this was the sturdiest and safest ship ever to sail in his fleet. To prove this, he announced that both he and the governor would sail on this ship until reaching the shores of the purported new land. Having little options available to them, the reluctant passengers agreed to sail with him on the old and seemingly dilapidated ship.

The first half of the voyage went smoothly. All three ships sailed in tandem, and the hopes of the passengers were buoyed by the freedom of the open ocean. The wind and weather was perfect for sailing, which allowed both crew and passengers to make good progress in the first few weeks of the journey. However, halfway into the journey the fall weather came and the ships sailed into a number of bad storms.

In one of the storms a ship sprang a few leaks damaging some of the stored food and the crew's living quarters located below the deck for the rest of the journey. In another storm, an artist came up onto one of the ship's decks to sketch the condition of the storm when the ship suddenly and severely rolled to the right causing her to lose balance and fall into the cold and raging ocean. Fortunately the crew were there to witness the accident and managed to save the drowning artist by tossing her a rope hanging down from one of the topsails just before she began to sink under the rolling surface of the water. When she grabbed the rope, the crew-members hauled her back up the side of the large wooden ship and then used a boat hook to pull her over the iron rail back onto the water-drenched and undulating deck.

The storms occurred on and off for a month making the end of the journey miserable for all the travellers. Many developed colds and the flu while other confined themselves to their damp and cramped quarters. To amplify the general discontentment, a few months had passed without a single sight of land.

Midway into the third month of the journey, tempers began to shorten until one of the passengers spotted land on the horizon and madly ran telling all the crew and fellow travellers. The news spread quickly and brought inexpressible relief and jubilation to all the travellers on the three weather-beaten ships.

The ships slowly sailed up the natural deep-water channel, and they let the ships glide into the shore so the captains could secure them to the large trucked trees that blanketed the shoreline. The eager passengers then shoved one another in an effort to be the first to run down the plank onto the sandy beach and take in the surroundings of their new home.

What they saw was mesmerizing. The land was so different than anything they had witnessed before, rendering the tribulation endured during the journey a dissent memory. They saw an endless virgin forest filled with a variety of trees and plants that would be ideal for building homes, furniture, ships, creating dyes for clothing, and providing fuel for consumption and trade. The surrounding ocean sea abounded with oysters and crabs, lobster, and several species of fish. The settlers could plainly see a gaggle of wild turkeys, squirrels, pheasants, and so many deer that it was difficult to see the trees.

Fruits, nuts, and berries also grew wild everywhere; and it was soon discovered that more substantial fare like peas and beans and corn, pumpkins, and squash grew naturally in the surrounding fields. As soon as every passenger reached the beach to view the landscape, each person instinctively knew that no one would go hungry again. They also instantly recognized that the long and natural coastline was ideal for fishing and exploring other areas of the land as well as trading with the populated and established kingdoms across the ocean.

The natural provisions of the land enabled the voyagers to prosper quickly. Trading ties had already been established between the new country and the merchant. As well, some of the crew-members were ordered to stay behind to help settlers build houses, till land, and gather supplies to stock the returning ships.

Within a year of their arrival, a number of small farms and businesses were established. The largest enterprise was fishing, but the fur and lumber trade was not too far behind. Households produced their own candles and soaps, and a brewery was built to make beer. A variety of sawmills and gristmills sprang up, and several shipyards were opened to build fishing fleets and a navy, which was psychologically important for the settlers who wished to avoid suffering any more brutal attacks that many had received in their homeland.

In all areas, the initial settlers built the foundation for a future success and predominance of the Republic. Among these are: the building of a strong navy and militia to be used in time of war; the establishment of new areas for trade; the discovery of precious metals and gems; and the beginnings of a large-scale manufacturing, agriculture, and, most importantly, a representative democratic government.

Finding the time and appropriate location to meet to discuss and codify the type and laws for the new country was not easy. Many of the residents were busy tending to their business, and the weather was too poor to host a large outdoor event until a local innkeeper suggested hosting the constitutional meetings at his establishment. It was large, warm, dry, and well stocked with food; and the rooms could be converted into separate meeting areas. With little hesitation, the location was accepted until the town hall was completed.

The hall was to be built in the centre of the community for both prominence and accessibility for all residents. Although a modest brick building, the hall was an engineering masterpiece, rivalling many of the elaborate continental churches. It sported a large clock tower, a reception room, a library, and a two-tired general assembly that was to be the focal point for all civic decisions in the new community. It also served as a schoolhouse until the building could be completed beside the hall.

Foremost in the minds of the new residents when devising their political system was to avoid the abuses experienced in their homeland. To do so, they ensured that each resident was to have an equal role in the formation of the government and the laws underpinning it, thereby making everyone the author and subject of the laws. This process was not as simple as any of the residents thought. There was a great deal of discussion and verbal disagreements. Few people wanted to compromise, and none wanted any one person to have more authority than the other.

In an effort to mitigate the growing tensions, a prominent member of the community suggested the creation of a rotating representational council composed of one hundred citizens. According to his proposal, the council was obligated to meet every Wednesday to discuss and vote on all the administrative affairs of the community. This included levying taxes, trade, and any possible declarations of war.

His plan was for the community to create and implement a fair and open legislative system that gave each citizen over the age of sixteen an equal and active voice in the government in the form of a formal governing council. The council, he proposed, was to be comprised of full-time representatives chosen by a rotating yearly lot process that gave a small stipend from the community to compensate for lost wages for the year.

He further explained to the community members that the names contained on the lot list were to be kept and updated at the town hall registry office so that when a man or woman turned of age, his or her name was added to the list. When it came time to selecting new councillors, the names of the citizens who had held office were to be indicated on the list and ineligible for the service until each citizen has had an opportunity to act as a legislator.

His plan also called for a statutory safeguard that stated that if the council found a proposed law to be unconstitutional, the proponent of the law was to be fined a substantial sum that would bankrupt almost any citizen. This safeguard was suggested to discourage frivolous ideas and glory seekers as well as ensure the accountability and responsibility of each councillor to the city and the constitution. Conversely, each law passed by the council became a legally binding law subject to the stipulated penalty if violated.

When he completed his proposal for the new assembly structure, the town hall congregation was silent. Every citizen was digesting and pondering the ramifications of his suggestions. After a long minute, an intense two-week-long debate arose among the attending citizens. Some indicated that they were concerned that they would lose their legislative voice and autonomy while others welcomed the opportunity to form a more efficient and effective government body that they felt retained individual participation and responsibility. In the end, everyone agreed to the proposal and appointed a town registrar to maintain and select the first council from the lot list.

Under the new governmental structure, the community continued to grow and prosper. The transoceanic trade brought both great wealth and new emigrants to the burgeoning city and, with it, significantly increased the population. The geography of the new land with its shoreline made it conducive to exploration, and the rivers helped spread the population north and south. Within ten years of its existence, new communities and settlements began to spring up in other regions of the vast land.

The distance between the new communities and the rapid increase in population made it difficult for the new communities to participate in the devised representative governmental structure. It also prompted several citizens to propose the formation of a delegation of representatives to discuss and arrange for a more centralized government structure. The meeting was also set to allow for the creation of separate community assemblies that administer and legislate policies in behalf of the community.

A notice for the meeting was proliferated and posted in all the communities established on the new land. The posters specified that all citizens were invited to attend and actively participate in the construction of the new structure. Also, in an effort to bridge the distance between the communities, the delegates agreed to host the meetings in a central location to make it accessible for all participants to arrive and to hold them in the late spring after the ice had all thawed and the flowers were in full bloom.

In total, 4,500 delegates took time off work and made the journey to participate in the formation of a national constitution and assembly. To maintain continuity with the existing structures and laws, the sessions opened with a review of the original constitution drafted by the first settlers to serve as the foundation and model of the new nation. After reviewing the constitution, the delegates were broken down into groups to make the decision-making process more manageable.

The groups were comprised of members from each community and were each charged with the responsibility of proposing constitutional enhancements that would facilitate the creation of a unified nation and adhere to the prevailing principles of self-government and democracy the communities had established.

The convention was scheduled to last three weeks with the addition of two weeks to be added if it was required to reach a constitutional agreement that was amenable to all the represented communities. All the groups were instructed to provide and document suggestions and, at the end of the first week, present them to the assembly.

The basic tenets contained in the final constitution framed the core of past educational curriculum from grade 3 to university politics 101. Given the marked change in the Republic from each of these tenets, I feel it necessary to enumerate them here or to highlight how far we as citizens have moved away from the principles that once made the Republic the envy and model of the democratic world.

The political arrangements established by the constitution were the result in large measure of the historical experience and the circumstances of the newly developed independent communities derived from their previous experiences and circumstances. Underscoring the experiences and circumstances was a coherent philosophy about the ends and means of government, which no delegate wished to deviate from. This philosophy of government was the espousal of three major political doctrines—individual rights, republicanism, and constitutionalism.

It is important to note to remember that the discussion of these issues was not limited to a small intellectual elite. Common knowledge of these philosophies was widespread. The challenge before them, as they understood it, was to apply the ideas to the circumstances of the moment and to transform the ideas into political reality. Central to the formation of a united government was the question 'What is the foundation of legitimate political authority?'

The constitutional framers held that the inalienable rights of individuals form the basis of all rightful governments simply by virtue of their humanity. Consequently any authority exercised by governments is exercised on the basis of the consent of the governed, and they consent to the exercise of that authority in order to acquire security for their natural rights to life, liberty, and estate. According to them, consonant with the original constitution, the only way political authority can be established and justified is through the consent and active participation of all individuals.

In addition to believing that political authority must be based on consent, it had to be organized in such a fashion that it could not be exercised in arbitrary ways. According to the framers, slavery consists in being subject to arbitrary authority while the liberty of political society consists in being subject only to the lawfully constituted and exercised authority to which we have consented. This notion of equality did not mean to claim that all people are the same; it meant that in spite of the differences, no one has an inherent right on the basis of some claimed superiority to exercise authority over others.

In addition to their belief in the philosophy of individual rights, the constitutional framers were firmly committed to the creation of a republic. In the minds of the framers of the Republic, republican government was synonymous with free government. Its major advantage is that under it, citizens are freer than they are under other forms of government. In their view, a free government that exists to protect the liberty of the citizens is inevitably much stronger than monarchical governments, which inevitably oppress their citizens.

They also agreed that while republican government was the best form of government, it was a form of government that was not possible under all conditions. Republics, both ancient and modern, had ordinarily been confined to small territories—territories that were much smaller than the expanded communities in the new land. The great accomplishment of the framers was their ability to find a way to establish the institutions of 'the extended republic,' a republic encompassing a much larger territory and many more citizens than any former republic previously had successfully done.

In defining the political foundations of the republic, the framers opted to maintain the previous devised representational system practiced in the founding community. In so doing, the Republic was to be administered by persons holding their offices for a limited and rotating period.

Finally, in addition to individual rights and republicanism, the framers were influenced in their deliberations by the idea of constitutionalism. Central to each delegate was the development of a written constitution that clearly codified a set of customs as well as clearly defined the relationship between the government and its citizens. More importantly, the framers shared the perception that a constitution exists not simply to describe the system of government, but its primary function was the imposition of effective limits on the exercise of political power.

The framers regarded the constitution as a higher law. It was to be that body of law that established the government, articulated the rights of the citizens, and was not to be violated by the government. It was to stipulate what the government could do and how it could do it.

However, when defining the political structure of the government, the framers recognized the need to go beyond the written codifications.

They felt that a mere piece of paper with rules and regulation written on it was an insufficient guard against possible violations and tyranny if the authorities of government were concentrated in one group. For this reason, they viewed the separation of powers and checks and balances as a requisite and an absolute requirement for a constitutional government.

They believed that only if the powers of government were properly balanced among the various branches in such a way that the exercise of power was effectively checked would a constitution actually guard against the arbitrary and improper exercise of political power. The checks and balances devised by the framers included the adoption of a three-branch administrative system comprised of an executive, legislative, and judiciary branches—each one to be checked and balanced by the others.

The executive branch was to be administered by a chancellor magistrate who was to be elected via a popular vote majority from all the districts in the Republic. The constitution specified that the chancellor magistrate could only hold office only for a two three-year terms. This limit was added to provide a check on the accumulation of authority from the public to the executive office. The constitution also assigned the chancellor magistrate the responsibility for approving legislation and the authority to declare war, negotiate with foreign nations, formalize commercial treaties, maintain an army, monitor the currency, maintain a national postal service, appoint constitutional judges, and levy taxes.

The legislative branch was given authority to propose legislation to be signed by the chancellor magistrate. The representatives were given the authority to hold office for three terms so as to have continuity between the chancellor magistrates but prevent the legislator from having a career. Each legislator was to be elected in the same manner and at the same time as the chancellor magistrate and to represent the sovereignty and will of the population. It was incumbent upon each legislator to consult with the district assembly prior to voting on a legislative proposal.

Important to the framers of the Republic was the creation of an independent and strong judiciary. An independent judiciary was extremely important to the constitutional framers to enshrine the rule of law established in the founding community. The framers regarded the rule of law as an important and mandatory safeguard to protect the constitution and prevent any possible corruption of the laws and freedom contained in the constitution.

The role of the judiciary took the framers the longest to determine because it was considered to be the branch of last defence—the one responsible for protecting the freedom of the citizens. In the end, the framers entrusted the chancellor magistrate the authority to appoint the judiciary with the check that the legislature could veto the appointment.

The appointed judiciary was the most unique of the central branches for its lifetime appointment. This rule was included by the framers to protect it from the caprice of elections and the turnover and appeal to public opinion they entailed. The judges selected were to be the most incorruptible, fair, and knowledgeable of the rules and spirit of the constitution.

The primary responsibility of the judiciary was to review legislation approved by the legislature and signed by the chancellor magistrate. It was to examine each law and policy to ensure that it adhered to the sprit and letter of the written constitution. Each judge was to review the legislation separately and present a report to the remaining judges for discussion. There was no time limit attached to the decision-making process, and no law was considered final until it received their unanimous approval.

To ensure that the chancellor magistrate could not violate the rule of law or overstep the authority granted to the position, the constitutional framers granted the central judiciary the responsibility of reviewing all proposed legislation for its constitutionality. If the law was found unconstitutional, it was to be immediately rescinded in a public address by the chancellor magistrate. In the same address, the chancellor magistrate was obligated to explain why he or she agreed to sign the legislation and apologize for the mistake. Following the apology, the chancellor magistrate was mandated to resign.

After the close of all the constitutional deliberations, the nascent republic was created supported by a written constitution and the separation of political power. The constitution contained the principles of popular sovereignty for all citizens and limited rotation in office by election, of trial by jury, of freedom of the press, of conscience, and of public and private assembly.

The political structure, geography, and distance formed foreign governments; and the abundance of natural resources enabled the newly formed Republic to flourish. Within a few decades of its formation, it had risen to be a major economic power, thriving democracy with a relatively strong military, capable of defending itself from foreign attack. Over the centuries, the political and economic success of the

Republic soon became a model for many other nations transitioning from the constraints of the monarchical government structure into free and democratic nations.

Despite all their foresight and built-in checks and balances, the framers did not anticipate the possibility that the citizens, legislature, and judiciary would willingly support the elected chancellor magistrate who openly violated the constitution and eliminated the checks and balances intended to limit the authority of the three branches of government.

I have no doubt that if they could have foreseen the future abuses of power and the violation of the constitution on those late spring days and evenings by the Oceanside, they would have taken more safeguards to protect the inviolable freedom of the citizens.

Unfortunately for the sustainability of the Republic, that responsibility rested in our hands.

THE EVENT

I can see the warden scuttling down the row of empty cells toward mine. Big circles of sweat are visible on his yellow short-sleeve dress shirt, and beads of perspiration were falling from his friar cut bald head onto to the floor large enough to create a small puddle behind him after each step he takes.

He has a grey folder tucked under his stubby right arm that looked like it is about to burst from the weight of its contents and spill over the cold cement floors. The weight of the folder caused him to walk hunched over and lopsided in an attempt to prevent the contents from springing out. Knowing I was observing him in this uncomfortable and demeaning position encouraged him to scuttle faster to reach the comfort and safety of his office.

This comedic scene was a welcome break from the tragic diatribe I was typing. I know that is inappropriate to laugh at others' discomfort, but his flagrant disregard for anything remotely resembling humanity made my echoing laugh extremely enjoyable. After I let it out, I realized how long it had been since I had laughed, which restored my sadness enough to ignore the approaching warden and divert my thoughts back to writing this story.

Finally it was the first of April. I had hardly slept all night. I was too excited thinking about the next day. I had been planning for this for well over a year, and I was anxious to know the election results. I knew that everything came down to the vote tally. No amount of pre-public polling in the months and weeks preceding the election or the generally accepted New Year's Day timeline that asserts that the candidate in the lead at the polls on this day will predict the final outcome of the national election was guaranteed—especially not in this election.

Many of my closest friends, professors, and colleagues told me that I was destined for a career in politics. I supposedly possessed the wit, rhetoric, looks, education, and public appeal. Although I love to participate in athletic and social activities and was on the debating team from prep school through my university career, I never really liked being the main focus of attention, which is why I opted to be the advisor rather than the politician.

I liked to be the ideas person and have someone else be the leader. I did not pursue fame in the traditional sense of having my name a household word. I just wanted an opportunity to implement my ideas and sit back and enjoy the success. That is why I chose never to run for election or participate in student government and political fund-raising activities. I was a background voice that did not want to see my face plastered all around town. I always found there was something a little soulless about being on every lawn, television, or highway billboard. Nevertheless, I loved the energy and rush involved in every campaign.

When I entered university, I was not sure what I wanted to do after my graduation. My parents had gone to university and had always taken it for granted that I would go too. Because I went to a private school and was surrounded by peers and teachers who held similar values as my parents, I hadn't even questioned the idea or considered other viable alternatives. Instead I just blindly set off to get a university education.

Before I could register for university, I had to select the courses I would study. This task was particularly difficult because I did not know what I wanted to study, and I had absolutely no idea what career I wanted. Looking through the course calendar, I placed a star beside each course that looked appealing to me; and I ended up with psychology, philosophy, sociology, politics, and history.

I selected these courses because I had a romantic notion that this is what one traditionally studied at university, and I vaguely thought that it would be fun and interesting to be a psychiatrist. My course selection irritated and disappointed my parents. They saw no utility in pursing a general arts degree and repeatedly asked me where that was going to get me. I had no reply except that they seemed like good courses, and I would decide later what to do with them. My only goal was to learn a few things and meet new people.

My first year was fun. I did well academically, played on the university soccer team, and met a number of new friends. However, academically I did not enjoy all the courses I was taking. In particular, I did not enjoy politics as much as I thought I would and I was not sure about psychology because there seemed to be more memorization than learning and I never appreciated multiple-choice tests, which all of them in my first year were.

The only thing I knew regarding the selection of my future curriculum for my unknown career at the close of my first year was that I was not going to take politics anymore. I made this decision because my politics course ended up being an introductory course in the history of the Republic and then a continuous lecture on legislation, party lobbying, and election procedures. At the age of nineteen, I found this type of information very tedious and boring and much too detailed for my abstract-oriented mind. Besides, I had already studied enough about the history of the Republic.

That summer, several of my friends planned a trip to tour around Asia and invited me to join them. I had always wanted to go there and welcomed the opportunity. My attitude was to always say yes to travel invitations because I had a life ambition to see the world.

Unfortunately my parents did not share my youthful ambitions. When I told them about the trip, they flat out told me that I was not allowed to go. The reason they gave was that my primary responsibility was to focus on school, not to go frolicking. Also, according to my parents, Asia was foreign and there were lots of drugs and danger.

I had learned fairly early on the inefficacy of arguing with my parents when they had made a decision. Doing so only resulted in a protracted discussion that inevitably ended in ill feelings and the impossibility of me achieving my desired end. Unlike other parents, my parents always agreed with each other, so the divide-and-conquer approach my friends employed was simply not an option. I had to be more creative and patient to persuade my parents to enable me to go to a particular party or, in this case, a trip to Asia. Being an only child also helped—somewhat.

I knew that it was not going to be easy to get them to agree with me taking a summer off work let alone travelling halfway across the world with a group of people and places they were, for the most part, unfamiliar. My parents had always regarded work as essential to building good character. Thus, despite our affluence, I was encouraged to have a summer job since the age of fourteen. If I did not work, I had to compensate by taking extra courses at school. Travel was something one did when one retired.

Having worked for five years, I wanted to tell them I was ready to retire but did not think this half-truth would go over well, so I opted for a more appeasing approach to secure my exotic summer trip to Asia. Still not having any notion as to what career to pursue after I graduated from university, I knew that selecting a professional degree would make them very happy. Given that I had selected to study arts course, I told them that I was going to apply to law school and become a lawyer.

However, though making them more supportive of my academic choices, it was still not enough to sway their opinion to support my proposed vacation. It was important that I pursue the topic while they were in an approving mood, so I also told them that on top of paying for the trip myself from my accumulated savings, I would take a full-credit commerce course that was offered in July and August when I returned. There was discussion, a pause, and then reluctant agreement with one condition. I was to call home every day to let them know I was safe. Without a second delay, I agreed to their terms and called my friends to inform them of my great news.

Immediately after completing our exams at the end of April, my friends and I set off for our two-month tour of Asia. Tired, hungry, a little annoyed, but also extremely excited, we arrived in Bangkok after a long thirteen-hour flight in economy class where meals and movies had to be purchased due to airline cutbacks. Asia was at our feet, and we had sixty days to tramp our way through it.

The whole trip was similar to a whirlwind and I have difficulty recollecting it.

Our primary objective was to see as much as we could in the short time that we had which meant that we did not stop long enough in any place to fully appreciate our surroundings. However, regardless of the pace of the tour, we got to see a great deal of ancient Asian architecture, visit and stay with some Buddhist monks, take a river ride down the floating markets, visit a wildlife sanctuary where we could sleep with the tigers and ride the enormous elephants, scale a mountain, climb the Great Wall of China, visit the Taj Mahal, and wander through old and mysterious temples.

Looking back now, I am so glad I persuaded my parents to let me go because it was one of the best experiences and memories of my short life. It is the only regret that I do not have. The major regret I do have was my decision to go to law school—not because I did not like it but because it is the catalyst as to why I am here today.

Writing and studying points of laws and how legal decisions affect political culture and understanding intrigued me. In law school, I spent a great deal of time in the library studying the constitution and all the legal decisions that had shaped the Republic since its inception eight hundred years ago. In fact, I enjoyed it so much that I decided to join the law journal as a writer and editor for the constitutional law section.

I worked at the journal office for all three years of my degree. I appreciated the easy access to the legal journals as well as the connection to the political and media world it offered. As the constitutional editor at the top law school in the country, I was frequently invited to social events that sported associates from the top law firms in the country, the federal judiciary, and the chancellor magistrate. Consequently when I graduated from law school, I was able to secure an articling job at the top constitutional law firm that was conveniently located in the capital city of the Republic—a place I had wanted to live ever since commencing my law degree.

Close to the end of my articling term, one of the firm associates decided to run for mayor after the current candidate had a heart attack and was medically advised to resign from the campaign. The election was to take place in six weeks, and she did not have a lot of time to begin and run a successful mayoral campaign. However, the incumbent mayor had done a poor job, and the opposing candidate had been doing well in the preliminary polls, which left a fair opening for her to fill. Regardless, his resignation had already given support back to the incumbent, and she was not well-known in the city, setting the stage for a tight and potentially exciting race.

I happened to overhear her intention to run for mayor while I was working late preparing a trial brief for the colleague she was telling her decision to. When I heard the statement, I lost all concentration on the brief that I was writing and began thinking of ways I could successfully run her campaign. I was so captivated by the prospect that I jumped back in my chair when she and the other associate came over to ask how the brief was coming along.

I was completely embarrassed. My face must have flushed a thousand shades of red, and it was impossible for me to hide the fact that I was entirely disengaged from the urgent brief.

'When will I be able to see the brief on my desk?' the associate asked, noticeably annoyed.

'In an hour, sir,' I replied apologetically. Then my heart began pounding; my hands began to sweat, and my stomach went into knots. I knew I had to finish the important brief and that I looked like a complete fool, but I also did not want to pass up the only opportunity I had to be her campaign manager. So, regardless of my anxiety and recent criticism, I summoned up all my courage and asked if I could be given the prestigious role.

The instant the words came out of my mouth, there was pause of silence while both of them were digesting the information. In the lingering silence that ensued, I thought that my aspiring legal career was over because no one was ever going to take me seriously again.

Thinking I was done and was going to be let go in the morning, I slumped back into my chair and tried to refocus on the trial brief. I could not look either of them in the eye for the fear of them seeing my humiliation.

As the seconds ticked on, my initial panic gave way to relief. I reassured myself that at least I had tried. Without that, there would be no opportunity at all. I also knew they were not going to fire me. The worse thing they would do is laugh at me and dismiss me from the firm after my term was complete. This reassurance gave me enough confidence to raise my lowered head up to match her eyes with mine. When I did, I was shocked to see her smiling.

My tense body instantly relaxed. *Everything was going to be okay,* I coaxed myself as I managed to return a coy smile. She stared at me for a moment longer, and then abruptly replied, 'That would be great. When you finish your brief, you can meet me in my office to discuss your plans to help me become the next mayor.'

The constitution of the Republic stipulated that candidates had to be elected by a majority of citizens. Thus, winning an election requires candidates to visit and convince the voting public that they were the best qualified and dedicated to represent their views. For centuries, candidates were able to campaign on their own behalf. They hosted events in the town halls, met residents at the local establishments, and organized debates with the opposing candidates to garner more community participation.

However, as the population in the towns and cities grew, it became more difficult for the candidates to meet each resident and advocate their abilities and values on their own. When this situation arose, candidates began looking for ways to positively present themselves without the burden of constant travel and interpersonal dialogue. To bolster popular support and policy recognition, they began to create and run advertisements in the local newspapers and streets for the local population to read and view the presented platform.

Initially the candidates did this on their own, but eventually they began to hire people to write and post the ads and campaign on their behalf. With the advent of modern technologies, such as the radio, highway and roadside billboards, and the television, a litany of entire staff was required to run a campaign for each tier of government. That is where I fit in. I wanted to manage the campaign messages, communication's medium, and staff. I wanted this position because I felt that it was the best way to participate in the policy decision-making process without being in the media and public spotlight.

I finished the trial brief as quickly as possible so I could meet and discuss my campaign strategy with the prospective mayor. Before outlining my rough campaign plan, I requested her to detail her policy platform. The meeting lasted into the early morning hours; but at its end, we had devised some effective slogans, snappy sound bites, and concrete policy vision messages to be delivered to the voting public.

Despite the lack of food and sleep, I felt amazing. In a matter of hours, I had managed to go from a lowly articling student to the campaign manager of a strong, intelligent, and capable mayoral candidate. At that point, I thought my life was perfect and that there was nothing that I could not do. In my extended elation, I failed to consider that some things should not be done.

I took to the task with great alacrity. I arranged to take some time off at the firm and to finish my articling term after the election. Having done so, I then met with all the television and radio networks to work out an advertising schedule and time slots. I also arranged rallies and speaking opportunities at schools and hospitals to gain media coverage and build the semblance of participation among the active city voters.

Overall, the campaign went very smoothly. In six weeks, the public opinion polls had swung heavily in her favour. The success was due in part to my ability to use the national media vehicles for candidate interviews because one of my close friends from the legal journal was an intern to write the news copy for the top news station in the country. When the internship expired, she was hired to assume the role of arranging guests for the weekend media press show that boasted a high rating of approximately fifteen million viewers.

Knowing this, two days prior to the scheduled election, I ask my friend if she could arrange to have my candidate appear on the weekend edition of the show. At first, she hesitated but then remembered that there was a twenty-minute vacancy on Sunday morning from a recent cancellation that could be filled with her. However, I would have to provide some background material to be used to draft interview questions of which I promptly gave to her. I also promised her a future undefined favour for her generosity.

The interview was an instant hit. The audience and normally stoic commentator were captivated by the prospective mayor's strong, assured, and visually appealing presence. At the end of the segment, she was asked whether she had any plans to run for the national legislature or not. In response to the pointed question, she merely smiled and coyly stated that her primary concern was becoming mayor and representing the needs of the capital citizens, and all future plans would be focussed around achieving this goal.

Regretfully I never fulfilled my promise of a future favour. In fact, I out and out reneged and disappeared in her critical time of need. It just so happened that she was the daughter of a third-generation immigrant, which placed her into the extermination category of the Immigration Act I drafted. It did not matter that she was a friend or that I had previously promised to assist her; I just blindly wrote the legislation.

In the legislation, all immigrants had been identified as enemies of the Republic and, therefore, to be arrested and eventually eliminated. My friend was only one of the many identified immigrants living in the Republic, and I hadn't even thought of her when I typed that fatal clause. When she received a leaked copy of the proposed legislation, she had left me numerous telephone messages to set up a meeting to discuss her situation all of which I erased and ignored.

On the day the death squads arrived, I was conveniently enjoying a European ski vacation. When I returned, the list of murdered names was waiting for me on my long mahogany desk to be signed and filed with the rest of the terminated terrorists. I shuddered thinking about my cool and insensitive cruelty—all in the guise of a political exigency. In many ways I was no different than the warden.

After the television interview, my candidate won the mayoral election in a landslide victory. Voter turnout was at its highest in decades and I was the happiest person. To show her gratitude for my role in her victory I was offered the job as a policy consultant for her office as soon as I completed my articling and passed the designated bar exams.

Like a puffed penguin, I elatedly accepted the offer and immediately returned to the firm to complete my articling term.

A year later I was approached by the incumbent chancellor magistrate to replace his campaign manager who, in his opinion, was doing a poor job and costing him key points in the popular opinion polls. I told him I would think about it and let him know in a couple of days. I was happy where I was and was planning another vacation as well as contemplating a marriage proposal, and I was not sure I wanted the interruption or the responsibility.

It was true. The incumbent chancellor magistrate was slipping rapidly in the polls and his campaign manager was partially to blame. The aired ads were mushy and lacked substance. None of the messages had any content, which had only reassured the voting public that he lacked both political integrity and vision. Meanwhile, the opposing candidate presented clean and straightforward ads that cleverly attacked the poor policy record of his opponent. With minimal effort his opponent was a solid sixty-five points ahead of in the pre-election polls at the time the incumbent chancellor magistrate made his request to me.

The opposing candidate's ads were true. The incumbent chancellor magistrate had a lacklustre record in his first term in office. He had not really enacted any policies and was seen more often golfing and meeting with domestic corporate giants who ran his companies while he was in office than in the legislative assembly. With his persistent, nonchalant attitude and lack of policy vision, it was not long before the citizens began to question their decision to elect him as the chancellor magistrate. Further from their minds was re-electing him to the esteemed and important position. Even I was planning to vote for the opposing candidate.

Caught up with his corporate meetings and daily golf games, the chancellor magistrate ignored the pulse of the Republic until his top advisor informed him that his ratings had reached an all-time low and his chances for winning the next election were extremely remote. Hearing this information and digesting its reality is when he decided to fire his campaign manager and approach me to assume the position.

He was incapable of taking responsibility for his own actions and decided to place blame on the campaign manager. I knew this, which made me all the more hesitant to agree to his request. On the other hand, I never turned away from a challenge and regarded the possible prestige as a viable reward if he and I were successful. I did this even though working for him would entail that I eschew my own political values to support his re-election.

If I could take any moment back in my life, it would be that one. It is not that I am entirely responsible for all the changes that have occurred, but I played enough of a role to be held accountable and responsible for the thousands of disappearances and anomie that have transpired since the unexpected catastrophe.

If I had not been at the helm and had not assisted the chancellor magistrate regaining political favour, things might have been significantly different, and I might not be sitting here writing this story and waiting to be executed for my crime against the Republic. However, all that retrospective is moot now because I did accept the offer, and I did write the ensuing legislation. There is no compensation but an apology that I hope one day cam be accepted.

The first thing I did upon assuming the role of campaign manager for the incumbent chancellor magistrate was create a new image for him that would resonate with the voting public. I knew the task was not going to be easy, but my conceit knew that it was also not impossible. This meant portraying him as a sincere man with vision and integrity and writing strong and pointed-messages speeches that would rival his capable opponent in substance and style.

Step one.

I also replaced all his political consultants. None of them had been doing a particularly good job raising his profile, and few of them could write. To replace them, I hired a team of general consultants from across the Republic to assist me in managing and preparing the overall campaign strategy, message and organization as well as to help with fund-raising, media, press meetings, and coverage. I then interviewed and hired a competent and experienced team of media consultants to write messages, prepare sound bites, pamphlets, radio commercials, and billboards for the overall campaign strategy.

Step two.

Because the chancellor magistrate had a dismally low public image, I had the media consultants immediately begin to create an extensive and candidate-friendly media list with the name and contact information for every newspaper, magazine, TV, and radio journalist from coast to coast. To successfully raise his profile and regain significant public support, I knew that it was imperative that the media be interested in the activities of the chancellor magistrate. This strategy proved to be extremely effective. Approximately one month into my tenure as campaign manager the voter pendulum began to swing in favour of the chancellor magistrate.

Step three.

I hired a web designer to help kick-start the fund-raising process and provide up-to-date public access to campaign information, voter issues, upcoming events, and success stories. The Web site also offered each visitor a chance to sign up and identify their top political issues as well as indicate what they would like to see implemented in the present and following term.

This strategy was the most successful in helping facilitate greater voter confidence for the incumbent candidate. It offered instant access to candidate information and a virtual space for political participation. Both of which conveyed the message that the chancellor magistrate was in touch and open to implementing with the political will of the people following the successful re-election.

The most difficult task I had was to formulate a communications and campaign strategy that would effectively gain credibility for the chancellor magistrate—a task that appeared almost insurmountable at the time. I thought that the best way to begin the image transition was to hire a ghostwriter who would write a biography of the magistrate to be available on the leading bookstore shelves within two months. The goal was not to make money but to get nationwide exposure and add weight to his dwindling reputation as a policy expert.

The book was a success and it was not long before the publisher was asking to print and distribute more copies and hire international translators. The book also secured national television interviews on talk shows and facilitated a nationwide book signing that resulted in a sharp increase in his public approval rating.

Step four.

While he was on the book signing tour, I also strategically arranged to have him and the campaign team visit local neighbourhoods, participate in community centre events, libraries, day cares, and attend education assemblies. Rallies were organized, and local media were informed and present at each event. Particularly integral to the credibility strategy was the traditional door-to-door visits where the magistrates' campaign team solicited policy suggestions and registered candidate support.

Step five.

The constant media attention and domestic outreach effectively removed the opposing candidate from the radar screen. His earlier strategy of highlighting the chancellor magistrate's litany of political and personality flaws began to get stale and appear slanderous to the unreceptive voting public. His biggest mistake was to try to run a campaign on what not to do, or what has been done, rather than what should and could be done.

With the increase in public confidence, I then turned the focus of the campaign to rebuilding strong political coalitions that had eroded over the last two years. I specifically urged him to downplay and limit his associations with his corporate friend and partners and look to align himself with national lobby groups and community organizations. This strategy would give him extra political support and lend greater votes on election-day because most people in the Republic belonged to or supported local political associations and lobby groups. The web of collations would then translate into a more unified dissemination of messages, raise money, and provide volunteers to solicit votes and plan local events related to the campaign.

The election messages fed to the voters were mere reiterations of their voiced concerns. Most voters articulated the need for more schools, a stronger economy, after-school programs for children, poverty reduction, health care, and personal security. As these are general issues, it was not very difficult writing communications and policy ideas to address each of these voter-raised issues.

Step six.

Due to the success of the collation building and interpersonal networking, campaign affiliate offices were established throughout the Republic—ran mostly by volunteers. I made it a mandate to keep each office open twenty-four hours a day with one day off a week to ensure that each volunteer had adequate time for personal and family activities.

Keeping the offices open was done to convey the message that all staff were busy and available to serve the needs of the community and keep the positive momentum going.

Step seven.

All the aforementioned campaign strategies brought the ailing campaign back to life. The Republic was uniformly transferring its support to the chancellor magistrate. The message of his success, outreach, and policy vision spread from coast to coast leaving little room for opposition interference. The campaign was ran in such a way that everyone we came into contact with, however briefly, was aware that the team and the magistrate were working hard, building momentum, and were ready to lead and win. Goal almost achieved.

Back to April 1.

The headline of the newspaper made me smile when my eyes scanned its bold letters. **Candidates Locked in Fierce Race**. According to the last poll, the chancellor magistrate was ahead on the election polls by the slim margin of 55 percent of the popular vote. I had done well to bring his rating back above 50 percent from its all-time low 40 percent approval rating one year ago.

I was anxious about the outcome but felt fairly confident that he would win the day. The local campaign officers promised to encourage all the citizens in their respective communities to vote, which, according to the numbers, would give our incumbent candidate 60 percent of the popular vote. This was more than I had hoped for, and a victory would assure a key departmental position.

The anxiety made it difficult for me to eat my breakfast. I could barely choke down the two pieces of multigrain toast and butter, and my daily glass of orange juice that usually disappeared in one sip remained untouched on my redwood table. However, despite my anxiety, I did manage to drink my ritual morning thermos-sized cup of coffee. I could drink this under any circumstance.

Without food, however, the coffee only heightened my anxiety as the caffeine worked its way in my empty and overtired body. When my hands began to moisten and my heart palpitate, I poured the rest of the coffee out and grabbed an apple and my pre-made avocado, cheese, and tomato sandwich from the refrigerator and deposited them absently into their designated spot in my black office bike bag.

Before leaving, I always washed the dishes mostly because I got home too late and did not want to do it later. Having a clean kitchen was important to me, and if I did not do them in the morning, I knew I would not to do them when I came home later.

As I was washing the four dishes I had used to hold my uneaten breakfast, I instinctively looked out the window to gauge the weather for the day. What I saw was not a good omen.

It was an ugly day that made me want to return to my cozy bed rather than ride over to the florescent bright and cold election campaign office. It was teeming rain and looked like it was threatening to snow. The sky was such a dark grey that it was difficult to discern that it was day. The weather had been terrible right across the country. Rain, snow, hail, and a hurricane had ravaged the Republic for a week.

The end of March and the beginning of April traditionally brought inclement weather, but for some reason, the weather on and leading up to election-day seemed abnormally bad. I shuddered. I did not want to go outside, and I especially did not want to ride my bike in that weather, but it was the fastest and most convenient way for me to get to the campaign headquarters.

I knew that if I did not want to go out, then most other people were probably feeling the same way. The communities showing the greatest support for the chancellor magistrate were experiencing the worst weather in the Republic—a situation that may significantly have affected the voter turnout and the election results. I tried not to think of any of these thoughts as I put on my rain gear, waterproof boots, and bicycle helmet. I did not want all the work I had done for the last eight months to be nullified by the freaky weather. I thought positively. If I were willing to venture out and brave the elements, others would too. *The Republic had a strong voting tradition,* I thought to myself. I opened the door and walked to the nearby post where my saturated bicycle was waiting for me.

I looked at my watch. It was just past 8:00 a.m. when I mounted my bike and began peddling through the waterlogged downtown streets toward the campaign headquarters. There were already a number of cars and pedestrians hustling through the streets in an effort to avoid the rain and arrive to work on schedule.

I was somewhat relieved to see the regular sea of people streaming through the streets adding life to the otherwise dull and depressing exterior atmospheres, but I did not appreciate the veritable tidal wave of splashes that engulfed me as the cars and buses sped past me. On any other day, I would have been highly irritated by the circumstances, but I was too focussed on arriving at the office and preparing for the polling stations to open that I kept my usual profane statements directed at the reckless drivers to myself.

When I arrived at the southwest entrance to the town hall park, I decided to take the ten-minute detour to get off the frenetic streets and ride on the unobstructed pathway. The normally smooth path was filled with deep and expansive puddles. In some areas, I had to remove my feet from the pedals and rest them on the angled metal bar connecting the top of my bike to the pedals. It was so wet that almost nothing was impermeable.

Regardless of the torrential weather, the diversion into the park was worth it. The early spring flowers were beginning to blossom contrasting an array of bright colours against the dark grey sky and the smell of the flowers also blended well with the thick rainy air to create a medley of intoxicating aromas.

The ducks, swans, and birds were all enjoying the weather. It was if each drop of rain added another toy to their natural playground. It was amusing to watch. Ducklings were learning how to swim, and the adults were flirting and frolicking in every surface of water, and those not in the water were all lined up in a procession heading toward the water. There were so many of them that I had to slow down and manoeuvre around the comical parade. I never liked riding slowly, but it was much better than staying on the drenched streets.

Coming up toward the northeast corner of the park, I could see the campaign headquarters. The bright blue-and-white signs depicting the portrait of the chancellor magistrate formed a border around the large front glass street window of the office. My heart raced, and I felt a strange hesitation in my mind and body as to whether I would proceed or not. It was almost as if staying there would stop everything else from happening. It was one of the first times in my life that I had experienced doubt.

The light turned green, and I shook off the momentary indecision and crossed the street leading directly to the headquarters' entrance. When I reached the entrance, I dismounted my bike and walked down the narrow alley toward the back entrance to lock my bike in the dry and safe storage room.

The room was full of boxes containing pamphlets and posters making empty space for a large bike a premium. I had previously cleared a spot for my bike in between two stacks of boxes, which everyone knew was my spot, but someone had forgotten and piled more boxes there making it more difficult to deposit my bike and hang my wet cycling gear to dry. The cramped space and being saturated with water added darkness to my already-dark mood.

I restacked several boxes and cleared a narrow opening that would fit my dripping mountain bike, removed my saturated outerwear, and entered the buzzing office through the back door. Everyone working on the campaign was already there. Some of them had slept overnight and had opted to stay and participate in the election-day activities.

Every computer and desk was occupied. The phones were constantly ringing, and there was barely a place to stand. The polls officially opened in two hours; and everyone was on high alert contacting volunteers, monitoring the pre-election coverage, and just staying busy to offset the tension.

I did not think I had much to offer in terms of support, and I did not want to interrupt the focus and adrenaline driving each team member; so I went over to the coffeemaker, poured a cup of coffee, grabbed a chocolate donut, and sat on the black leather couch facing the large-screen television. Staring at the screen, I could not really hear what the commentator was saying. It didn't really matter; it was all just speculation until the votes were cast and counted. However, it did serve as a slight distraction while I watched the clock and waited for the chancellor magistrate to arrive.

I thought that it was odd that he was not there yet, but I had only arrived, so there was the valid possibility that he was also running late or did not want to come too early to avoid the pre-polling office drama.

Around noon, all the campaign staff and volunteers and I began to get noticeably worried and concerned. The polls had been opened for two hours, and the early numbers were quite close. The vote tally was not necessarily indicative of the future outcome because most voters were at work and would cast their ballots in the early to mid evening. The real concern came from the continued absence of the chancellor magistrate.

I had attempted to call him a few times to find out when he was expecting to arrive but had been routed directly to his voice mail each time. I left a few messages and received no reply. I tried to act nonchalant about the situation to lower the growing nervous tension in the office. As the minutes ticked by, this already-difficult task became more difficult for me to accomplish because I think I was the most stressed person in the entire team.

When the polls opened, there were no more phone calls to take. It was illegal to call voter after voting had commenced. The only ones working were the computer monitors watching and reporting the early results of the Internet voting. The rest of us were huddled in front of the television strung out on coffee, sugar, and insomnia—watching, waiting, and checking our watches and the door for signs of the still-absent chancellor magistrate to arrive.

At this time none of us were listening to the commentator; we were too anxious. It all we saw was a bunch of talking heads that occasionally blinked. Consequently, when the emergency broadcast came on replacing the monotone drone of the election announcers, we were all in disbelief; and most of us took a few seconds to register the fact that the television screen had changed and we were now witnessing a national catastrophe.

Shortly after the end of the Second World War, scientists and government officials in the Republic opted to employ the ability to use the same theory and technology that had been used to build and explode the first nuclear bomb to create high-power nuclear-power-generating stations. The stations were supposed to be highly efficient and significantly reduce the cost of producing and delivering electricity. It was also theorized that nuclear power would allow the development of cheap, compact, long-lasting power sources that would continue generating power in any type of weather conditions.

When the first project was developed, there were a number of protests. Against the building of the nuclear facilities based on the human and environmental degregation that could occur if one of the reactors malfunctioned. The scientists assuaged their concerns by informing the nation that this new form of power production was economical, environmentally clean, and safe. Demonstrations of its effectiveness were conducted throughout the Republic, and gradually the majority of citizens felt more comfortable with its use.

For nearly sixty years, the nuclear power stations ran by the national utility company offered uninterrupted, safe, and inexpensive electricity to every residence in the Republic. During this period fear of radiation, safety, and security had all been erased from the memory of the citizens.

Over the years, the design and technology used in the nuclear-power-generating stations had changed and become less cumbersome to build, and by the time of the event, the Republic housed over twenty-two generating plants that accounted for 65 percent of the power generated in the Republic. On April 1, at 12:01 p.m. and 12:15 p.m., two of them were obliterated in front of all our watching eyes and gaping mouths.

We all sat numb, incredulous, and horrified at the spectacle that unfolded in front of our innocent faces. Suddenly and without any sound, we saw the Republic's largest nuclear power station bathed in brilliant light, as if somebody had turned the sun on with a switch. Then the station appeared kind of flat and colourless like scenery seen from the light of a photographic flash. The light appeared to remain constant for about one or two seconds and then began to diminish rapidly.

We all looked at each other in terror then turned our mute attention back to the white screen. After what seemed like minutes, we saw an eerie shape that resembled a large red ball connected to the ground by a short grey stem. The ball rose slowly, lengthening its stem and getting gradually darker and slightly larger. Then a structure bigger and brighter slowly became visible making the ball look somewhat like a raspberry. Then its motion slowed down, and it flattened out but still remained connected to the ground by its stem, looking more than ever like the trunk of an elephant. Then a plumb of white smoke ascended from the concrete stack rising into the sky like a volcano slowly penetrating the highest cloud layers.

Just when we all thought the explosion was over, a white patch on the underside of the cloud layer just above the explosion suddenly appeared. The patch spread very rapidly, like a pool of spilt milk, and a second or two later, a similar patch appeared and spread on another cloud layer higher up. The eruption of smoke clouds then dissipated and was followed by a long rumbling, not quite like thunder, more regular, like a large training rumbling through the destroyed landscape of the power plant.

None of us had time to digest the situation when we were immediately diverted to another emergency taking place 1,200 kilometers from the original blast. The image on the screen had just changed on time to display a massive fireball burst out of a reactor and blow off the next reactor's heavy steel and concrete lid.

The first explosion was then followed by a second and more dramatic and powerful blast shot burning lumps of graphite and reactor fuel into the air. These lumps landed in various places causing many fires. In all, the explosion had created a crater with burning graphite and about thirty fires in other places around the plant.

Police and firefighters could be seen rushing from every direction to secure the area and attempt to put out the fires. Nuclear waste emergency units sent to measure the extent of the physical and environmental damage also arrived to provide protective suits, masks, and gloves to the attending police and firefighters.

The news camera kept its focus on the firefighters entering the remains of the destroyed nuclear complex. Far inside the edifice, screams from surviving workers could be audibly heard through the announcer's microphone. Suddenly one hundred people—burnt, charred, with missing limbs, and intact—appeared on the screen in their mad attempt to exit the contaminated and unstable building.

The television screen conveyed chaos as the surviving workers fell over each other on their way to the relative safety of the open air. When they appeared outside, there was a loud rumbling sound flowed by a tremor that sent debris flying and the south reactor to implode, crushing a group of police officers that had just finished securing the area. Dust, smoke, and debris clouded the air. It was difficult to see anything through the camera than ghost-shaped bodies falling and getting up to run.

The cameraman then panned to a shot of a firefighter carrying a person on his shoulder out of the smouldering complex. As they got farther out of the building and away from the suffocating fog of debris and radioactive smoke, the image presented on the television screen became clearer. The former white anti-radiation uniform of the firefighter was now charcoal black with smatterings of red that looked like someone had splashed a can of bright red paint on him from a distance.

The person on his shoulder was a woman whose body was completely burned. Initially it was difficult to discern the gender because all her hair was burned off, and it seemed as if her eyelids had also been burned off. When the firefighter placed her on the ground, she scrunched up in fetal position with her head a few inches above the ground in her condition.

The reporter asked her if she was okay while handing her a blanket. Almost inaudibly she said yes because she was one of the lucky ones.

Immediately following her response a medical crew rushed over placed her on a stretcher, and rushed her over to the medical lab on wheels. In the meantime, the same firefighter had disappeared back into the burning building.

All of us in the campaign office watching the gruesome and apocalyptic events unfold were speechless. There was nothing any of us could say. It was as if we had entered another dimension and as if we closed our eyes long and hard enough, and when we reopened them, life would be back to normal. None of us dared to imagine that it would get worse.

The reporter then located a member of the nuclear waste emergency unit to ask how the explosion occurred and what the prospective damage was. The nuclear spokesperson was noticeably shaken and did not remove his obtrusive mask when responding to the questions. He advised the reporter and news crew to leave and wear protective clothing. He also informed all the onlookers and community residents living in a two-hundred-kilometre radius of the explosion to evacuate their homes and area immediately.

He then went on to explain that the amount of radioactivity in the atmosphere was one hundred times the amount dispersed from the atomic bombs dropped on Hiroshima and Nagasaki. He also informed everyone that it was the same situation at the other nuclear power station that exploded.

He informed the nation that cumulatively both explosions had killed more than two thousand people immediately and that the number was likely to dramatically climb when the medical officers diagnose the cause of death from acute radiation sickness, burns, tumours, and cancer from breathing in the contaminated air, drinking water, vegetables, and livestock. He then reiterated the need to evacuate the surrounding communities immediately.

In addition to the two thousand casualties, approximately fifty police officers had been killed from falling wreckage and small explosions. A report had just been issued informing the emergency response team that all firefighters battling the fire from the reactor building had died, totalling 187, and many more had received life-altering and threatening injuries from other areas of the buildings. He then concluded by saying that the two power plant explosions were a cataclysm that would be permanently etched in his mind for the remainder of his life.

While the nuclear specialist was responding to the reporter's first series of questions, the reporter had heeded his advice and clothed himself in the radioactive protective gear. Seeing the two men dressing in white uniforms with black gas masks and large black protective gloves and boots in front of a burning building and decimated building was a veritable scene from a horror science fiction movie that did not intend to have a happy ending.

The next question the reporter asked was the one everyone one in the Republic wanted to know—what caused the two power-generating plants to explode? There was a marked hesitation, and one could notice that he did not want to respond but knew he needed to respond. The entire Republic was watching and needing an explanation to the diabolical and unnatural events.

After gathering the diplomatic words in his mind, he slowly answered. 'It appears,' he said, 'that both explosions were caused by the overheating of the main reactor that created a nuclear meltdown.'

'It is conjectured,' he continued, 'that the reactor was able to overheat because the emergency core cooling systems were manually immobilized. The immobilization of the cooling systems then caused the steam pressure in the system to gradually increase, which induced the cooling water to be brought to a strong and steady boil.

'When the water was at the peak of its boil, the power generation was increased causing more steam to be generated, which inevitably led the roof being blown off the reactor. Once the roof was destroyed, the reactor was exposed to the outside air that in turn caused the white hot graphite in the reactor to catch fire and release large amounts of radioactivity nearly one thousand meters up into the atmosphere.'

'Do you have any idea how this situation could have occurred within minutes of each other in two different plants build in different years and operated by different organizations?' the reporter pointedly asked.

'At this point, it is only speculation,' he continued diplomatically. 'However, coincidence and safety violations have been ruled out. It is impossible too for the same accident to occur by the same cause at approximately the same time. All the power stations follow the strictest safety codes, and the employees are trained to deal with any emergency. There were no tests or safety experiments planned for today at either plant, which leaves us with no other rational explanation than to attribute both events to internal sabotage and an act of terrorism.'

We all gasped. *Could it be true?* we asked ourselves. *It must be true,* we answered ourselves. The nuclear expert was right; there was no other rational explanation. It was a shock to every citizen. An external or internal enemy had never attacked the Republic, and the words sounded like two trains crashing at full speed when they reached our innocent ears. Simultaneously everyone realized that we were vulnerable and the fact that we could be subject to attack at anytime from anyone. In one tragic instant, the golden age of the Republic came to a full stop.

While the event was unfolding and the expert being interviewed, all of us in the office had been completely focussed on the images emanating from the television screen that none of us had noticed the chancellor magistrate enter the office. He had been sitting on a desk behind us for nearly an hour and had not said a word.

When the expert announced that the tragic explosions were the heinous acts of terrorists, he calmly said, 'We need to write a press release and arrange a press conference. I must address the nation and let them know that the situation is being addressed and the Republic has a strong and competent leader they can trust to guide them through this dark emergency.'

When we heard his voice, all of us jumped out of the couch in fright. We hadn't expected anyone to be there, and hearing him talk without being able to see him while our attention was entirely diverted felt like a terrorist was in the room. The surprise of his presence quickly dissipated as his words sunk in, and we immediately got to work writing a speech and arranging the press.

While I was trying to calm my whiling thoughts and compose a reassuring speech, the chancellor magistrate came over, put his bony hand on my shoulder, and thanked me for all my dedicated work on his campaign. He also assured me that he appreciated everything I had done to improve his image, approval rating, and policy vision. He then continued to inform me that I was a key component to his success and that he highly desired to retain me on his team as a top political advisor.

I thanked him and said that it had been fun, and I looked forward to working on his team after we won the election. He paused, removed his skeletal hand, sat down on the desk, and looked at me in the eye and coolly said, 'There is not going to be an election.'

I blinked incomprehensibly.

'We are in a state of emergency,' he continued undaunted, 'and we must act quickly and decisively. Any change of leadership now shows a vulnerability and gives the terrorists power. The election must be cancelled until the crisis has been resolved.'

It took me a moment to fully comprehend what he was saying. When I finally understood, I nodded in agreement and went back to writing the speech. Here is what I wrote:

> The Chancellor Magistrate: Ladies and gentlemen of the Republic, today we have all suffered and participated in a national tragedy. Two nuclear power plants have been sabotaged and caused nearly three thousand deaths and thousand more in causalities in a terrorist attack on our country.

> In response to the attacks I have arranged to have emergency teams dispatched to assist the victims and their families as well as to charged our security units to launch and conduct a full-scale investigation to hunt down and incarcerate those inhuman creatures that committed this heinous and unprovoked act of terror on our peaceful and free nation.

> PAUSE

I want to send a message to the terrorists, if you are watching and not killed by the blood of your own hand, we will find you and will not tolerate you. Our republic has no room for terrorism and will not house any terrorists.

We have taken all appropriate security precautions to protect every citizen of the Republic. Our military and police are on high alert, and I have taken the necessary security precautions to continue the regular administrative government responsibilities. I will meet with my opposing candidate to postpone the election so that we can all get through this day of shock, pain, and tragedy that has befallen our beloved Republic and move into a safe and secure future that is free from terror.

A toll-free victim hotline has been implemented to enable individuals to anonymously report any information they know about the acts of terror committed against our people and the Republic today. I know that it takes courage for people to step forward in situations like this, and I urge anyone with information that may be useful and helpful to authorities to use this opportunity.

Fellow citizens, today's attack were a declaration of war against every citizen and our republic and our values. I want to assure you that the search is now underway and will not cease until we have found all of those responsible for these terrible acts.

No distinction between the terrorists who committed these acts and those who harbour them will be made. The terror and fear they have sought to inspire will not come to pass.

Our republic stands for freedom, acceptance, fairness, and openness. These are the very values that the terrorists attempted to destroy. We recognize our own values are sacrosanct and resolute. We shall prevail over this tragic day of darkness.

Today we will grieve, mourn, and attend to our lost friends and family care for the wounded. Today and henceforth, we will fight to combat and thwart all planned acts of terror on our sacred soil.

The members of the legislature join me in condemning the attacks and offering our condolences to the families and friends that suffered a loss. Your loss is our loss. With your d assistance we will hunt down, punish and eradicate all those who dared to transgress our hallowed nation.

Let us take a moment of silence to remember the victims and wounded.

Silence

END

THE NEW REPUBLIC

T he bright hot sun is receding into the horizon bringing with it a welcome cool breeze. In a few hours, I will have to retire my writing and wait for the morning—if I make it to the morning.

Waiting is the worst part. Knowing that one is going to die is surprisingly, not difficult to accept—perhaps because it is something we all know will eventually happen.

Knowing how one is going to die is more difficult to digest.

Of all the ways I imagined dying, burning was not one of them. I was hoping for a more abrupt and instant death such as a heart attack or a stroke. Something instantaneous and most suitable to my cowardly personality. I did not have to be asleep I just wanted it to be fast. All of those thoughts are gone and moot now. I now know that my death with be both slow and painful and it is a waste of time thinking about it because there is a very good possibility that for me there may not be a tomorrow and I still have much more to write to complete the tragic tale.

The attack on the nuclear-power-generating stations resulted in nearly 2,500 deaths, hundreds of personal injuries, and an uncountable number radiation related illnesses. In an instant fear and insecurity spread its tendrils to every resident of the once free and peaceful Republic.

Only days after the event the early warning signs of the beast of paranoia that slowly and methodically destroys rationality, peace, and human interaction. All of which helped contribute to the ensuing nightmare to the once-venerable Republic.

As the dust settled in the affected regions of the nuclear explosions, the citizens of the Republic were left for a few days to ponder what the attacks meant for the nation. The task of comprehension was made more difficult because there was no historical precedent from which to compare. Other nations had been the subject of such attacks and incidents, but they were explainable by civil conflict or acts of sabotage in a time of external war.

On April 1 the janet@docustar.co.il secure and thriving Republic was violently jolted out of its complacence and security by an unknown and faceless attack on its own soil. With it brought widespread fear that was compounded by the fact that no one knew who the enemy was or the reason for the attack. That the only known thing was that such acts could happen anywhere at anytime by anyone.

Because of this uncertain feeling, no one felt safe and spent the next few days with the constant expectation that another and far-worse calamity was going to occur. Everyone wanted to find out who was responsible to bring some closure to the nightmare and the possibility of returning to a normal life.

The act of terrorism was also a shock to the rest of the world leaders.

Immediately after the event, each world leader held a special televised news conference condemning the attacks and offering their condolences. None of them imagined or thought to attribute the attacks as originating from any of their own citizens, and none could conjure why anyone would want to attack the Republic.

The attacks were so shocking that it facilitated a world history watermark. It was the first time that all of the disparate world leaders agreed with each other. Within an hour of the reported attack every leader broadcasted a televised message offering support and sincere condolences to the Republic as well as a full-out condemnation of the attacks and the perpetrators of the attacks.

However, for some unknown reason, the media in the Republic did not run the heartfelt and sincere condolences offered by the world leaders in regards to the attacks very long nor did it allow for the citizens to return to their normal lives. Instead it fuelled the fear and sense of loss and horror by repeatedly airing the explosions on television twenty-four hours a day. Not a single station could be tuned into that was not covering the story or re-casting the tragic event.

The Internet news sites were re-broadcasting the expositions scenes twenty-four hours a day along with running interviews with the victims and bereaved family members Recounting their shock and horror experienced witnessing the tragedy and losing close friends and relatives.

Wherever one went or looked there was a reminder of our vulnerability, of the pain, insecurity, that the attacks created among the populace of the Republic. More disconcerting to the general citizenry was the knowledge that the orchastrators of he attacks were free to roam the streets, eat at the local restaurants, shop at the local supermarkets, and play at the community centres with their children.

The mounting fear and anger, partially fuelled by the constant bombardment of the devastating images flashing across every available screens and the lack of suspects, inspired a number of people in the affected communities to report that they had witnessed suspicious behaviour from some of their new neighbours on the days preceding the event. These unsubstantiated reports were hungrily picked up by the media adding to the tension and causing more reports of suspicious behaviour to flood the understaffed terrorist-prevention hotline with tips and accusations of their neighbours and colleagues across the country.

It was the policy of the terrorist hotline to take each call seriously, and within days of the alleged attacks, several people were arrested and detained for questioning regarding their knowledge of and their relationship with the terrorists. Each of the arrested individuals were eventually released and declared innocent, but the stigma and suspicion in the community toward these people remained.

The more time that elapsed before someone was charged and convicted of the conspiracy to commit terrorism, the more the anxious the populace became. The general anxiety wasn't attached to any particular person or thing; it was motivated by the desire to renew the bond of trust and freedom of movement that the explosions had violated. Because the event had been so unreal, and apparently unprovoked, most people shared the belief that if the group of terrorists were caught and convicted, the terrorism and possibility for future attacks would disappear. Unfortunately this relief never came.

True to his word, following the cancellation of the election, the chancellor magistrate assigned me the prestigious role of his personal political advisor. When I heard the announcement I could hardly believe my ears. The good news almost made me forget about the horrific events I had just witnessed and allowed my imagination to wander freely over which policies I could write and help enact and how I would be a key figure in leading the nation into a prosperous, safe, and secure future.

Shamefully, in a twisted way, I was grateful that the tragic explosions had occurred. I had some grave doubts about the outcome of the election and I was beginning to wonder whether or not I had made a mistake leaving my job at the mayor's office to become the campaign manager for the chancellor magistrate. It is true that in the opening months of the campaign we had made great headway in passing the opponent in the opinion polls, but in the crucial weeks leading up to the election the opposing candidate had climbed back in the polls to make it a tight race.

For the most part, the chancellor magistrate was aloof and dispassionate about the domestic and international affairs of the Republic. However, he had an insatiable need for recognition, approval, and authority. To him, being the chancellor magistrate was the pinnacle position. It meant that he had the final say in all legislation and the ability to appoint judges and to render constitutional decisions. Above all, it meant that he was the most important figure in the Republic.

When he had come to me to request my assistance in running his re-election campaign he was fairly humble and concerned that he had lost the disfavour of the citizens and would in all likelihood lose the election. He regarded me as his only hope and promised a good financial return. I have never been motivated by money, but I have always sought after the opportunity to shape affairs and formulate policy to create the ideal state.

This quest is why I could not refuse the position to be his campaign manager and why I felt like a child in a candy store having the reigns to draft and advise legislation on how to run and improve the Republic. It is also why I felt some perverse joy about the attacks on the power plants and why I belong in prison for crimes against the state. From the moment I accepted his Faustian offer to become his personal advisor I became complicit in the destruction of the Republic.

Drunk in the trappings of my new position I wilfully chose not to think about the consequences of my actions. I did not want to question the merits of the chancellor magistrate's information or openly criticize his method of administration. I blindly accepted the fact that the Republic was in a crisis and needed firm and sound decisions from strong leadership. I wanted to be the person to lend the advice. The chancellor magistrate knew this and gave me his full confidence knowing that I could write speeches and propose legislation that would maintain his position.

As a result, when he asked me to write a speech on the state of the Republic and to include a large section on apprehending some terrorist involved in the explosion, I complacently complied. Writing is never an easy task, and the more information one has the easier it becomes; so to write about the apprehension of the terrorists, I asked him to provide me the details involving the arrests and names of the assailants to lend the speech more effect.

I realize now that when I received the information that some terrorist suspects had been arrested I did not feel relieved or gain a greater sense of security. A part of me even resented the fact that another election would be called and my current position would be in jeopardy. I did not want to have to go through the hassle of organizing the campaign again after it was so close to being over. I decided that despite my desires to remain an active part of the chancellor magistrate's administration, I would decline the post of campaign manager and return to my previous position with the mayor.

In retrospect, I need not have been concerned, or more poignantly, I should have been extremely alarmed. That is the problem with wilful ignorance. One can turn one's critical thinking capacity off to justify one's own ambition and personal schema, and that is exactly what I did when he handed me the papers detailing the activities of the alleged terrorists, the nature of the arrest, and the reason for their attacks. There were pictures, life biographies, plant diagrams, records of phone calls, electronic messaging exchanges, and a detailed plan of how they were going to attack the two power plants and a copy of a confession. It was all very neat, tight, and seemingly official so much so that it seemed like it had been fabricated by a movie producer.

The interesting thing about the arrested terrorist suspects were never seen or interviewed. They just simply disappeared after the speech was given. The public did not care because they had a greater sense of security, and the chancellor magistrate appeared to be completely competent and in control of the Republic. The real problem came down to whom the alleged terrorists were and the possibility that there might be more.

I have already noted that there are several moments in my life that I wish that I could retract; that speech was one of them. The speech confirmed the success of the economy and the strengthening of international relations. It also detailed the positive and proactive measures that have been taken by the government to assure the safety and security of all citizens as well as thanked each person for their courage and community support in a time of national crisis.

The speech also gave a powerful address on how the citizens and the Republic showed the world and the terrorists the internal strength of character and zest for freedom on which the Republic was built and defended daily in the hearts and actions of every person. The tone then changed to offer condolences to all those who suffered loss and sustained serious injuries during the attacks. Then it mentioned that the terrorists had been caught.

I have provided the most important parts of the speech for you to read

> . . . The police, with the assistance of the military and the flood of information that was received on the terrorist-prevention hotline from the conscientious citizens, led to their discovery. The group had been living in the communities and working at the attacked plants for three years. The bodies of the terrorists were found two days ago under the debris during the investigation of the explosions. When the police searched the residence of the primary organizer, they discovered a confession letter detailing their involvement and culpability in the power plant attacks.
>
> PAUSE
>
> The confession stated that the terrorists were proud of their actions, and if they had any chance of surviving the nuclear explosion, they would plan and perpetrate another attack. The reason for the attacks was their dislike of the values and international reputation that the Republic had that rendered

it immune to attack. They categorically stated their dislike of freedom and multicultural acceptance.

PAUSE

The confession also states that they were sent there to politically and physically destroy the Republic because it has corrupted the other nations in the world with its preference for peace and freedom . . . .

Then the real blast came.

The speech moved on to outline the origin and nationality of the alleged terrorists. It said that they were immigrants from a small and bellicose nation that had been excommunicated from the international community for its policies and practice of torture, tyranny, and civil and international terror. Furthermore, it stated that the nation refused to abide by international treaties and sought every opportunity to develop and trade weapons to sell on the black market. The nation is purported to have initiated, funded, and supplied over thirty-five civil conflicts in the last ten years.

I begin with the instructions:

LONG PAUSE, STEP BACK FROM THE PODIUM, BIG SIGH, AND RETURN LOOKING NOTICEABLY DISTRAUGHT.

It is a sad day for the Republic to discover terrorists living and plotting to destroy the fabric of the Republic and kill thousands of innocent citizens for the diabolical reason of envy, hatred, and desire for war among the law-abiding and freedom-loving citizens. It is almost unthinkable.

PAUSE

When I heard and saw the unadulterated information in my hand, I did not want to believe it. I actually had my intelligence and policy sources verify the data and dental records of the remains. When I received the validation, I cried because it was true, and it meant that our open borders were no longer safe.

REMOVE HANDKERCHIEF AND PLACE OVER THE EYE AND OUT, HEAD DOWN IN A FIVE-SECOND MOMENT OF SILENCE. PUT HANDKERCHIEF BACK INTO POCKET. GRAB THE PODIUM DETERMINEDLY WITH BOTH HANDS AND CONFIDENTLY LOOK DIRECTLY INTO THE FACES OF EVERYONE IN THE AUDIENCE.

What I am about to say is the most difficult thing I have ever had to say. The reality is that our beloved Republic is no longer the safe and the impenetrable bastion it was only seven days ago. Terrorists have taken advantage of our centuries-old open-border policy and generous immigration policy granting immediate work visas to all persons who take the journey to find refuge in our vast, bounteous, and free lands.

READJUST HANDS ON THE PODIUM.

The terrorists have entered our land, live in our communities, and work beside us.

TIGHTEN GRIP, LOOK DOWN, LOOK STRAIGHT UP AGAIN

These values are not our values and will not be accepted or tolerated by the administration or any citizen.

PAUSE.

I have made it the mandate of my emergency administration to restore peace and security to every citizen residing in the great borders of the Republic. This will not be an easy task, but it is a necessary one. There will have to be changes made to our immigration policy to ensure that those entering our esteemed Republic possess the values and policies required to live and work peacefully in our lands.

Achieving peace and security and continued prosperity I solemnly pledge. Terrorism and the terrorists will not be tolerated.

Thank you.

At the conclusion of the speech, the entire legislative council gave the chancellor magistrate a standing ovation that lasted five minutes. It was later reported that several viewers actually wept. I was elated. It was the first speech I had ever written that produced such a profound effect on an audience. I drank in the approval and enjoyed the accolades at the evening dinner party. The champagne never tasted so sweet and I was firmly established in the chancellor magistrate's office.

At the close of the speech, the media swarmed the chancellor magistrate hurling questions on the appearances and family of the deceased terrorists—who had given them the assignment, where they were living, did they have any friends, and did they leave behind a detailed copy of their plan? The chancellor magistrate calmly answered all the questions. He informed them that no pictures existed of the terrorists because they wanted to keep a low profile. They did have their names and addresses and a detailed sketch of their terrorist plot and who was involved and their roles at the respective nuclear facilities. He said the records would be released to the media later in the day.

The story of the uncovering of the terrorist plot and the discovery of their remains in the ruins of the power plants was the top news story for a week. Each story would begin with a view or description of the two explosions and then move into psychological discussions on the background of the individuals, their motivations, and the repercussions of the open-border immigration policy.

Several television networks tracked down displaced residents of the evacuated communities and employees of the power plants to discuss their knowledge and memory of the terrorists. In the interviews, the terrorists were identified as crafty, creepy, and loners. They were also described as the people who kept to themselves and did not participate in community activities. They were also reputed to have not taken care of their houses or appearance. One shopkeeper noted that they were seen buying suspicious material at Reno home centres and hardware stores as well as purchasing books on nuclear physics.

The employees described them as introverts who stuck to their jobs and did not associate with the other staff. They were accused of spying on certain employees and lurking around in special access areas without proper access passes. When the director of the second power plant was interviewed, she said she was suspicious of them from the beginning and would never have hired them.

She explained that she had tried to give them the benefit of the doubt, but their personalities and surreptitious behaviour made her and every other employee feel uneasy, like they were always being watched without being able to see the watcher. She stated that she was planning to terminate them the day of the disaster.

The public and media ate up the stories. The more they were printed and broadcasted, the more real and plausible they seemed. Within a few months after the disaster, books were written on the psychology and activities of the unidentified terrorists that became instant bestsellers the minute they were placed on the shelf.

The stories, analysis, and barrage of books and articles all served to lend credibility to the chancellor magistrate's assertion that the terrorists had been apprehended and that they did exist. Both facts had a twofold effect on the citizens of the Republic. Most of the citizens felt relieved and comforted that the terrorists had been discovered and, better yet, were dead. No one wanted to be subjected to a trial that gave equal weight to the defence. In everyone's eyes, they were guilty, and everyone thought they should be dead.

The desire for criminals to be executed was not a judicial practice exercised in the Republic and was universally believed to be a malicious and inhumane punishment. Consequently, most people were happy they did not have to face the trial and the desire to execute the architects and performers of mass destruction and mass murder.

The second and equally important effect the discovery of the terrorists on the populace of the Republic was their statement that others were available to continue the work. The perpetual possibility of an unknown and devastating attack from a co-worker or neighbour was highly unsettling and it was not long before people began to limit their conversations with strangers and be inviting to new neighbours. The change in attitude was subtle, but its effects were widespread. I was to find out later that the horrific event and its fearful outcome was everything the unelected chancellor magistrate and his invidious administration could have hoped for. Enter the policy planner—me.

The first item on the chancellor magistrate's administrative agenda was to legislate tighter immigration policies. The policy was justified as a required response to the fact that the terrorists had been identified as immigrants and had taken advantage of the open and porous borders to plan and enact their heinous crimes. The policy was also in reaction to his promise to protect the Republic from any future terrorist acts.

The Republic did not have a formal immigration department because its unwritten policy was to accept all immigrants who expressed a real need to become naturalized citizens of the Republic. The only real policy on immigration was the administrative ability to place limits on the number of immigrants permitted to enter in a given year. However, this clause had only happened twice in the Republic's long history for economic exigencies. On the whole, the number of immigrants had been stable enough to maintain a free and open policy. For the first time in over eight hundred years, the Republic was about to draft its first official immigration policy.

Because the Republic did not have a formal immigration department the task for drafting the immigration policy became my portfolio. The new policy I was charged to write came specifically from the chancellor magistrate. He provided the content and material that was to be included in the policy and I was to write it for presentation to the legislative council. In drafting the legislation, I merely incorporated his requests and once again did not question its ethics or repercussions. I did not think it was my role to question his authority but to carry out his policy vision and ideas.

The new policy was far-reaching and marked a significant change in the accessibility and procedure for immigrants to successfully enter and take up residence and work in the Republic. The first part of the new law called for the provision of border patrol officers at every access point into the country.

The Republic did formally have customs officers and some police officials located at each border entry point but did not have any real immigration officials or controls at these areas. To account for this shortfall, the policy called for the creation of a former border patrol service to be hired and supervised under the new immigration department. When passed, the border patrol were mandated to work closely with customs offices and local police forces in the region to ensure that no immigrants could pass through the border without first meeting with an immigration official.

In the past, immigrants were simply asked to fill out a form available at the border entry points and provide an address when they would be residing in the Republic and allowed to proceed. In the new policy, all identified immigrants were required to report to the immigration officer stationed in the border patrol office for questioning and registration.

The immigration officers were given the authority to interview, question, and deny immigration to every candidate. The questioning was to be done individually and lasted up to three hours without food or water to make an uncomfortable and stressful environment for the prospective immigrant. The harsh conditions were devised to provide an opportunity to have the immigrant state inconsistent answers and expose hidden agendas for immigrating to the Republic.

The policy also mandated the immigration offices to detain and search all belongings and persons suspected of plotting to commit acts of terrorism in the Republic. If any information was found or discovered in the search, the officer was to report it to the border patrol unit that was instructed to arrest the suspected immigrant and escort them to the local border patrol office for further questioning and searches that could last several days.

During the course of the search if the border patrol officer discovered evidence of intent to participate in a terrorist activity or an intention to deceive or the Republic, the detained immigrant was immediately arrested and imprisoned for an indefinite period of time. The justice officials permitted this treatment towards immigrants or visitors because the detainees were not a citizen and therefore were not subject to the same laws governing criminal law detailed in the constitution.

The policy also stipulated that the same treatment and questions be given to each immigrant to render the immigration process transparent, fair, and impartial. In the first passing of the legislation, each immigrant that successfully passed the new immigration process was given the same freedom that all previous immigrants had upon entering the Republic.

Once drafted, the policy was presented to the legislation council as a necessary act of the Republic to prevent future terrorist acts and strengthen the security of the Republic to ensure peace and stability for each of its citizens. When the vote was taken, the proposed legislation was passed unanimously with minimal debate, and the immigration department was formalized.

The new immigration policy had the effect of significantly reducing the number of immigrants coming to the Republic. When the news of the policy reached the international community, few families and individuals from foreign nations wished to go through the arduous and lengthy immigration procedure.

Internally, the legislation was positively received.

The majority of citizens reported that since its implementation, they felt more secure and pleased that the interim administration had created a border patrol and immigration department to monitor and stymie any attempts to enter the vulnerable Republic illegally. Most citizens also indicated that they felt more comfortable knowing that all immigrants had to pass through the rigorous entry procedure before they could gain access to live and work in the Republic.

The relatively recent immigrants to the Republic had the opposite feeling. Far from feeling secure and protected by the new onerous policy, they felt threatened and targeted as a potential internal menace should any other terrorist plots be uncovered. Many immigrants reported that they were concerned and slightly distressed that their relatives might not successfully be able to join or visit them in the Republic. They also expressed concerns that the policy could easily be extended to targeting the immigrant residents of the Republic.

The response to the articulated concerns from the administration was that only those who had terrorist connections would express concerns, which resulted in the formal interrogation of the interviewed immigrants. Regardless of the outcome of the interrogation, those immigrants were entered into a tracking database, and none of their family members were permitted to even visit the Republic.

The new immigration policy also placed greater restrictions on visitors entering the Republic. Each tourist was expected to provide adequate and acceptable proof of his or her visitor status. This included passport checks that registered the name, age, sex, country of origin, and length of time visiting the Republic. All of this provided data was immediately entered into the newly developed immigration database for future reference and terrorist identification.

At certain high-volume border entries, this process could last up to two hours depending on the length of the line by a border patrol officer. Any visitor found entering or leaving the Republic with an expired passport stamp was immediately arrested and incarcerated in the same fashion as the suspicious immigrants.

Anticipating the potential targeting or possible role as a scapegoat in the instance of another catastrophic event, many recent and naturalized immigrants began to form coalitions to combat ethic stereotyping and unlawful search and detainment. In less than a year, several immigrant lobby groups had been formed and were actively meeting, protesting, and researching ways to counter what they deemed to be unfair and derogatory legislation.

The immigration lobby groups had a lot of support from lawyers, student groups, and individual citizens who supported the diverse, open, and accepting foundation of the Republic. These groups and organizations sent in a number of petitions calling for an election. The opposition leader had strategically positioned herself on the side of the lobby groups and ran her platform on the need to amend the immigration policy as well as to return to the democratic process of holding a legitimate election.

The discovery and deaths of the power plant terrorists had set the Republic at ease, and the peace of the ensuing months brought more force upon the administration to amend the harsh immigration and visitor legislation. Many citizens felt safe and have regained their initial confidence that made the Republic so attractive as a model for students of politics and newly created democracies around the world. A year had passed since the horrific acts, and there was a unanimous appeal for an election to ratify the administration.

In response to the lobbyists' efforts, media coverage, and national appeal for an election, the chancellor magistrate held a press conference on the day of the anniversary of the power plant explosions to address the immigration policy and to set an election date. He began the press conference thanking the nation for their bravery and cooperation in stopping the terrorist threat. He confidently informed them that if it were not for their vigilance and determination, more terrorists might have attempted to follow in the footsteps of the April 1 attackers.

He then went on to explain the effectiveness, fairness, and continued need of the aggressive immigration legislation. He explained that nearly one hundred immigrant claimants had attempted to illegally enter the Republic. He then praised the immigrant officers for detaining and uncovering evidence that led to the arrest and conviction of twenty immigrants conspiring to enter the Republic to carry out acts of terrorism and violence upon the infrastructure and the citizens of Republic.

The speech also emphasized the importance of the legislation to prevent terrorism and its proven record of maintaining peace and stability in the Republic. It acknowledged that the policy was stringent, but frequent surveys indicated that both affected groups welcomed the minor inconveniences because they knew that they had nothing to hide and knew that after the process was completed they were entering a country that was safe and secure.

He then clearly and confidently stated that the freedom and security of all immigrants residing in the Republic was important to the current administration. The intention and limits of the policy was to protect and isolate legitimate immigrants from the terrorists. He then repeated that the only people who should be concerned about the components of the immigration policy were the terrorists themselves.

Last on the press conference agenda was the announcement of the election. Elections were traditionally held on April 1; but due to the special circumstances, and agreement with the opposition leader, the election was to be held on October 1, thereby giving each candidate six months to plan and launch their campaign.

Announcing the election on the date of the anniversary of the attacks gave each citizen a surge of patriotism and faith in the incumbent administration. In the early months of the campaign, he enjoyed popular support, which placed him several key percentage points above his competent opponent. However, his lack of domestic policy vision and introverted personality soon began to lose him support in the crucial months leading up to the election.

My role as the minister of the Department of Immigration prevented me from acting as his campaign manager. In my stead, he had hired his friend and corporate colleague to run the campaign. His campaign manager was as short-sighted and distant with the electorate as he was. The continued distance and lack of future policy vision offered by the office of the chancellor magistrate soon resulted in a precipitous decline for his re-election in the polls.

This decline gave fuel to the immigration lobby groups. None the groups were appeased by the assurances given to them by the magistrate in his anniversary press conference. In fact, a number of them became more alarmed.

Many of the lobbyists considered the chancellor magistrate's closing remarks in his election speech to surreptitiously imply that the immigrant lobby groups were associated with the terrorists. It was this association that they found most worrisome.

To fight what they considered to be an underlying attack on all immigrants, several immigrant lobby grouos were formed to raise awareness and support for defeating the incumbent chief magistrate. Seeing an opening, the opposing candidate made a backroom promise to tye lobby groups to rescind the legislation if she were elected.

The public denunciation of the immigration policy by the immigrant lobby organizations and the opposition candidate's promise to withdraw the policy is what eventually led to the electoral victory of the incumbent chancellor magistrate.

One month prior to the election I began to get concerned about my employment. The prospect of the chancellor magistrate being re-elected looked remote, which ostensibly meant that I would be unemployed. I very much enjoyed my position as the minister of Immigration but thought it would be prudent to de-align myself with the plummeting administration and look for opportunities outside of the national political sphere. During this time, I spent more time researching employment options than supervising the new office. For the most part, the department was auto-functioning and did not require a great deal of top-down direction. It was bureaucracy at its finest.

I honestly think that most departments could continue operating the same way for years in the absence of directors and ministers. Most departments are entities on their own that take on a perpetual motion on their own. The only time a senior official is required to be present is to propose and implement a policy change; otherwise, I posit Senior management is entirely superfluous in the day-to-day management of bureaucratic affairs. Of course, once again, I was wrong.

Two weeks prior to the election, I elevated my job search. I had narrowed it down to five prospects, and it was my intention to contact them all in the afternoon. I felt even more motivated to start my search when I read the newspaper headlines. **The chancellor magistrate's popular vote had dropped to an astonishing 20 percent.** It is the lowest rating any candidate has ever received in the long history of the Republic.

Yikes, I said to myself, shaking my head in disbelief. It was almost pathetic. In a mere five and a half months, he had dropped 50 percent points to effectively carry the mantra as the biggest loser of all time. With a week left, it was very possible that he was going to drop even more.

The thought of being associated with such a candidate ruined my day. I wasn't very confident that any of my selected prospects would be interested in meeting with me. I was almost angry. The whole situation seemed absurd and impossible.

After reading the headline, I sat dejectedly in my office stewing about my pending unemployment when my phone began ringing. I did not want to answer it as I was in the process of closing off files and actively engaging in the mental preparation to leave the job. I did not want any more responsibilities, and I did not want anyone to know I was planning to leave.

I let the phone ring three times before I answered it. I decided that talking for a few minutes was better than having the red light blink in my face or for me to have to listen and potentially respond to the message. When I answered the phone, I barely had time to say my name and hello when my ear was assaulted by the excited words of one of the immigration officers. She said that the border patrol spotted and arrested several suspicious individuals who attempted to illegally enter the Republic by water. The suspects had several pounds of explosives, guns, and military gear in their possession. Also in their possession was a detailed list of places they planned to destroy, the first of which was the national legislative building.

She also reported that under questioning, the captured terrorists said that the attack on the legislative building was planned for the following morning, but they did not say by whom or what time. They also made it clear that they had internal support and the attack was not going to be stopped in their absence.

With my heart racing, I asked if the chancellor magistrate had been informed. She responded yes and replied that he was personally going to meet with the terrorists to get more information from them. Partially stunned, I hung up the phone. I began to draft a press release and inform the Republic of the immanent threat of another terrorist attack from a radical immigrant group with strong internal ties. It was also my responsibility to evacuate the legislature and the surrounding buildings and put extra military and police patrols in the area.

The ensuing terrorist alert snapped the Republic out of its renewed complacence. There was panic everywhere. Everyone went home and waited in fear for the news report to display the next national tragedy. I was equally shocked and did not know what to think.

For the most part I was on autopilot. It was my responsibility to ensure the borders were secure and to guarantee that all immigrants and visitors entering the Republic were valid and not a threat to national security. In an instant all thoughts about future job prospects were forgotten and my full attention was given to monitoring the border operations.

I did not sleep. I stayed at the office all night waiting for reports and updates on the terrorists and the security of the legislature. No one was allowed to enter the legislature and the military guards were posted around the perimeter of the building as well as strategically placed in adjacent buildings and sewer systems. The entire Republic was on high alert and none of us wanted to witness another catastrophe.

At approximately 7:00 a.m. the next day the chancellor magistrate called to say that the terrorists had provided all the information related to the list of attacks, and all people involved had been apprehended. He thanked me for my diligent efforts and asked me to prepare a press conference to inform the distressed nation that the terrorist's attacks had been adverted. Much relieved, I composed a brief message and called the local networks and papers to send representatives to the legislature at 8:00 a.m.

The press briefing was short and assured in tone. It thanked the hard work of the border patrol, immigration officers, and Immigration Department in identifying and preventing a terrorist attack. It then thanked the citizens for their courage and resolve in another time of crisis.

The short speech specifically stated that the primary mandate of his administration is to severely punish all terrorists and their associates. It reaffirmed the goal to make the Republic safe, secure, and terrorist free. It also stated the need for strict legislation and internal vigilance to identify and prevent terrorist activities. Finally, it demonstrated the efficacy of the immigration policy and the effectiveness and ability of the current administration to combat terrorism and protect the citizens of the Republic.

The terrorist alert and its subsequent prevention by the chancellor magistrate had a profound reaction throughout the Republic. Within a day, his approval rating jumped to 80 percent. The tide also turned against the immigrant groups who openly opposed the immigration policy, making them a target for personal insult and personally ostracized at work and in the neighbourhoods for their potential affiliation with terrorist groups.

Because the opposition candidate had campaigned almost solely on rescinding the immigration policy, she lost nearly all national support except from the increasingly alienated immigrant organizations. In a strange twist of political fate, her popular approval rating dropped 85 percent, replacing the chancellor magistrate as candidate to receive the lowest approval rating in the Republic.

With virtually no time left to reorganize her campaign platform, and minimal time for the chancellor magistrate to lose his recent rise in national appeal, the election results were not a surprise to anyone working on either campaign. At the end of the count, the incumbent chancellor magistrate won by the greatest vote differential in the history of the Republic. To all of us there was no doubt that the terrorist threat on the nations two largest nuclear power plants had been a great boon to his campaign.

However, at the time, the reason for the victory did not concern me.

What mattered was that I was going to continue to be a key person in deciding the future of the Republic for another five years. Knowing this, his now assured victory made me almost giddy and more supportive than ever of my political benefactor, regardless of his ill-intentioned policies he wished me to draft and implement.

Following his inauguration the chancellor magistrate held a ten-day policy-planning retreat. The purpose of the retreat was to propose policy legislation and structure for the new Department of Republic Security.

The mandate of the new department was to prevent future terrorist attacks and protect innocent citizens from the deadly terrorist activities. The national republic security legislation composed at the retreat gave widespread authority to the central government—authority well beyond what our constitutional framers would have endorsed. It gave the chancellor magistrate the authority to use the military and law enforcement agencies to periodically subvert freedom with the aim of enhancing internal security.

The national security legislation enhancements included the authority to run random surveillance checks on telephones, interactions, and postal communications; monitor and arrest participants in protests; establish a DNA database for all criminals and immigrants; expand the terrorist-prevention hotline; and create a new internal security enforcement unit as well as the ability to search homes and seize materials potentially related to the commission of terrorist acts and to prohibit antigovernment material, speeches, and rallies.

Furthermore, the legislation enumerated harsh penalties for protecting and meeting with suspected terrorists. Its policy stated that any person who knowingly aids and abets a terrorist planning or carrying out act of violence is considered a terrorist and subject to the same penalty accorded to terrorists—arrest and detainment without trial for an indefinite period of time.

The Republic had been formed in response to a tyrannical monarchy. Close to the hearts of the framers of the constitution was the prohibition of despotism in the Republic. Paramount for the constitutional framers were the importance of the rule of law—that no one is above the law, not even the government—and a split in responsibility and role between the judiciary, legislature, and executive magistrate.

For several hundred years, the Republic thrived under the rule of law, supported by the split in governmental authority. The rule of law, the authority of law, ensured legal autonomy from politics and religion, which successfully made it a regulator of government power, equality before law, and procedural and unbiased dispersal of justice. Because the laws created had to be approved by all three levels of government, the citizens were freed from the ills of arbitrary laws and abuse of position, thereby ensuring the greatest degree of freedom for each person residing in the Republic.

The legislature passed the Department of policy with only ten dissenting votes. According to the checks and balances contained in the constitution, before legislation can become legally binding, it must have the full consent of the judiciary.

Traditionally when there was legislation or proposed legislation that a segment of the population disapproved of, they would organize public rallies, distribute literature, and, if necessary, arrange and participate in protests.

At all times freedom of speech and of assembly in public and private spaces were sacrosanct constitutional values. In fact, it was considered a political obligation to voice one's personal opinion so that others could hear and judge the merits of the argument. For this reason, students and other citizen lobby group rallied together to plan and participate in a nationwide protest against what they considered to be unconstitutional legislation. The protest organizers wanted to plan a large event to get maximum media coverage and to send a message to the judiciary who were in the process of examining and ratifying the legislation.

The protest was arranged to be a two-day event in the capital. Approximately eighty thousand protesters flooded the relatively small city, booking up all available hotels and camping in the park. The administration was aware of the large-scale event and had put up security barriers around the legislation, chancellor magistrate's residence, judiciary, and Republic military headquarters to prevent any terrorist insurgents.

Using the new authorities and privileges stipulated in the recently passed security legislation, the protest became a massive security operation, and the city was literally turned into an armed camp. All available police officers were dispatched to monitor and control the protests with substantial military support. The incessant hum of helicopters could be heard all day and night as they circled the city and photographed the protesters from a bird's eye view.

In all, there were 3,000 police officers; 8,000 military personnel; and approximately 1,500 more military personnel stationed at headquarters for possible deployment. Each police officer was clad in black uniforms and helmets and carried large bullet-resistant shields with exposed nightsticks poised to attack any nearby protester. Additionally, each of the law enforcement officers was equipped with water cannon, attack dogs, tear gas, and guns loaded with rubber bullets.

For two days, the streets of the capital were wet with a continuous stream of water, and the air poisoned from the perpetual volleys of tear gas canisters upon the stationary crowd. The tear gas was so pervasive that one could not walk down the street without eye protection and the air was tinged yellow. Residents living several kilometres outside of the downtown area where the protest was concentrated complained to their local political officials that they felt imprisoned in their homes because every time they dared to go outside to water the garden, walk the dog, or perform an errand they could feel the sting and inch on their skin and the immediate burning in their eyes both of which were intensified when they attempted to cleans the caustic layer from their infected skin with water.

Prior to the start of the protest inmates from the nearby prison were transferred to provide ample space for the potential incarceration of any identified antigovernment and terrorist supporters participating in the protest. Custom and immigration officials were also instructed to question and detain anyone whom they remotely suspected of planning or supporting terrorism, and a curfew from dusk to dawn was imposed to keep the street cleared at night. Any violators were to be immediately arrested and incarcerated at the nearby empty penitentiary.

The massive security measures rendered it impossible for most of the protesters to remain outside to convey their message of dissent in solidarity as planned. The few, who did try, ended up being arrested and detained in the local penitentiary well after the protest was over.

During the demonstrations several protesters were beaten bloody by the nightsticks carried by the hired officers, and seven people were shot and killed while running from the immobilizing spray of the water cannon. Every protester was photographed and documented and eventually targeted in the database for removal and conspiracy to commit insurrection. I found out later that my housemate was among them.

The size and magnitude of the protest garnered a lot of media attention. The news of the tear gas, beatings, arrests, and killings received national coverage. The apocalyptic images displayed on every available television swayed public opinion over to the protesters.

The disorderly events, beatings, and killings at the hands of the security enforcers forced the chancellor magistrate to make a public address on the excessive use of force on the protestors. He wanted the speech to portray him and the security law favourably, so he personally requested that I write the speech, of which I eagerly agreed. All the blame was placed on the protestors, not the brutal force used by the law enforcers. It did not matter to me whether I believed it or not, only that the public did. This is what I wrote:

> Chancellor Magistrate: Fellow citizens, the events of the last weekend are unfortunate. It is never pleasant to read or see a law enforcer hit, maim, or kill a violator; and I apologize that you had to witness the measures required to maintain and promote security and preserve freedom at the protest. Threats to our freedom have occurred, and it is important and our duty to enhance our ability to respond to these threats. In responding to the threats, we at all times acknowledge the values and practices of the Republic.

> PAUSE

> Our goal is to promote good governance and protect citizens and our fundamental freedom. I assure you that all the actions taken over the past two days have been done to protect these sacred freedom and values.

> Each of those injured, killed, and arrested were found conspiring to commit terrorist acts and attempting to escape. If it were not for the resolve and intelligence of our nation's

law enforcement units, the security of the legislature and military complex would have been breached.

Grenades, dynamite, smoke bombs, layouts, and stealth communication devices were discovered on each of the injured, killed, and arrested persons. It was not the will of the officers to inflict harsh measure upon these individuals, it was their duty, and they and this administration stand by their courageous actions.

PAUSE

The peace and security of the Republic can only be ensured through the conscientious strengthening and respect for the rule of law. We will continue to implement policies that enhance our ability to prevent, mitigate and respond to terrorist activities. In so doing, we recognize the cultural and economic contributions made by immigrants to the Republic, and we are committed to ensuring respect and providing legal protection, safety, and security to every resident.

Thank you.

The address assuaged many of the concerns the citizens had regarding individual freedom to assemble and to speak and the unnecessary use of force. The threat of terrorism weighed heavily on most of the citizens' minds. Consequently, when the chancellor magistrate mentioned that evidence related to terrorism had been discovered on the victims, the tide changed to support the law enforcers' actions and the new security legislation.

As I stated earlier, the judiciary was charged with the critical responsibility of validating that all legislations conform both to the intent and content of the constitution. There were several controversial areas of constitutional non-compliance contained in the security legislation that in all likelihood would be struck down by the judiciary. If this were the case, the actions taken against the protesters by the police, military, and immigration officers would be illegal and subject to a trial. The chancellor magistrate would also be required to make a public apology and resign from office.

The drafters of the anti-terrorist legislation hoped that the exigencies surrounding the legislation would be considered by the judiciary and passed without amendments. At the time of its creation, there was a fifty-fifty chance of gaining their approval. The protest events made the outcome more uncertain.

It was a tradition that the judiciary travel in the same vehicle to render all their constitutional decisions. The chancellor magistrate was to follow behind, and the legislative representatives were all to be in attendance when the judges and chancellor magistrate entered. This was done to give the judiciary prominence as well as ensure that everyone was present when the decision was rendered.

The day of the decision began as usual. The weather forecast was unseasonably nice. It predicted a mostly cloudy sky with sunny breaks with reasonable temperatures. The decision was to be telecast at 10:00 a.m., and the vehicles would be coming down Capital Avenue around 9:30 a.m.

As usual, I was sitting in my office with the television on. At 9:30 a.m. sharp, the media cameras honed in on the stretch black limos driving down to the legislature. I had the television on mute because I did not care for the announcer. I was also rather bored. There is nothing more inane than watching cars proceed down the road for fifteen minutes.

Realistically speaking though, it was a monumental event. The judiciary had never taken this long to decide on the constitutional merits of proposed legislation before. The ramification of this decision also had far-reaching consequences. It is for this reason that I had the television on before the 10:00 a.m. scheduled announcement.

I picked up the newspaper and turned to check the soccer standings. My increased workload had prevented me from watching the weekend matches. I also had to take a temporary leave from my recreational team that made me a little grumpy. When I looked back at the television, I thought that I had accidentally hit the remote and changed the station to the movie channel. I was about to re-enter the channel when I saw the chancellor magistrate being carried out the car on a stretcher and put in an ambulance. I then noticed that the car carrying the judiciary was in flames and we could see its former occupants mangled and decapitated body parts scattered across the treelined road. To create another televised national horror.

The minute it happened my phone was ringing with reports from the terrorist hotline, which was flooded with information and suspects. Within minutes, the security officials arrested and detained everyone participating in the protest stationed along the route as terrorists.

All that went through my head was that the Republic was in a crisis. The judiciary had been murdered, and the chancellor magistrate was in the hospital. It felt like Armageddon. I collapsed in my chair, composed myself, and then hurried over to the hospital. My deputies could field and analyze all the reported tips and suspect information. I would go through them when I came back. 'Arrest them all' was what I said when I left the building.

Miraculously the chancellor magistrate was unscathed. His car had been far enough behind to avoid the brunt of the explosion, and he had only suffered minor contusions and cuts. When I saw him, he was remarkably composed and determined to have the judiciary render their requisite decision on the legislation.

I told him they were all dead and the decision had to be postponed. He hesitated and then stated that the murder of the entire national judiciary exacerbates the need to ratify the legislation. Lifting himself up on the sterile hospital bed to give himself an appearance of strength he coldly stated that the constitution granted him the authority to appoint the judiciary, and that was exactly what he would do.

Noticing his projected passion, he recollected himself and slowly slid down the white bed to resume lying on his back restoring his vulnerability then quietly stated that despite the terrible loss, the decision would have to be made because the legislation was too important to remain in abeyance and he was not going to allow the terrorists to stop the legal and political process of the Republic.

True to his word, within three days, eleven more constitutional judges were appointed and given a week to examine the security legislation before rendering their verdict. In just three days, they declared that they were all in agreement to render their decision. This time, there was no car procession. Instead the military officials—through underground tunnels linking the Republic's military—national court, and legislation assembly escorted the judges and chancellor magistrate. Before a packed house and the national media representatives, they individually announced their decision. The verdict was unanimous. The legislation was constitutional and was officially ratified to become law.

It almost went without saying that the terrorist attack on the judiciary propelled the Republic into permanent panic and terror. Anyone who looked suspicious—immigrant, criminal, or citizen was reported to the newly formed Department of National Security that I was now the appointed director.

In a year, I was to draft the mandatory DNA-badge legislation. In two years, I created and supervised the hiring of the security and sanitation units that effectively made the Republic a virtual prison for every resident.

Every action, word, or twitch was surveyed, thereby making each citizen his or her own jailor. Every action was public. Higher fences had to be built to have a modicum of privacy. Each person was rendered immobile. Any movement or interpersonal association beyond work and the basic means to preserve one's biological processes was a life-and-death risk. In this state it was difficult to distinguish between the living and the dead. Colleagues, neighbours, friends, and family would disappear before one's eyes—vanishing as if they were never there. It was then that names became to be regarded as liabilities and superfluous.

I did not have the same concerns. I had a government badge, which gave me immunity to the terrorist hotline. I also was the minister for the Department of Internal Republic Security. I did not need a fence or be concerned about walking down the street or talking to someone. I was free, or at least I thought I was.

Watching the chancellor magistrate that day at the hospital, I had a revelation. I realized behind the uncontained smile that there had been no terrorists. The only terrorist was the chancellor magistrate who had hired and organized the horrible events himself so he could maintain his position. At the time, I did not know that there was someone more sinister behind him. I found that out later Regardless when I left the hospital, I did know that the terrorists were straw men created to frighten the voting public into supporting his well planned dictatorship.

I did not just stumble upon this revelation before I came here. I knew immediately after I exited the hospital room. I knew when I was drafting all the anti-constitutional DNA legislation. I knew when my best friends were arrested and burned in the local crematorium. I knew it and I did not care. I had decided to stop thinking, to not judge, and just do my job. I had willingly become deaf, dumb, and mute.

Unfortunately, so had everyone else.

THE INTERROGATION

The full moon was rising higher in the sky casting a welcome pale white light upon my trembling and tired hands. A cold chill was running through my aching body creating an almost feverish state. I knew it was not going to be much longer for me. I would make it to dawn at the latest—if my body could hold up. The only benefit I had was that he was monitoring me and wanted to ensure he placed my live, feeble body into the glowing embers of the awaiting furnace himself. Oh, what glee it would bring him. Well, I would acquiesce. There will be no point in fighting. It will almost be welcomed. That is the emotion he wanted; it would be easy to give but not before I finished writing. I urged myself to continue writing.

Write I urged myself on.

I felt my body weakening. I decided that it was time to summon the interrogation. I knew that my body could not hold out any longer from the daily regimen of torture, fatigue, and poor nutrition. I felt that if I waited another day before participating in the interrogation, I would not be mentally adept to answer the litany of pointed and attacking questions.

Knowing that it was the last day made it easier for me to endure their perverse pleasure inflicting another round of sadistic and gruelling torture on me. Not so enjoyable was allowing the warden observe my submission.

He will be overjoyed at the prospect of breaking me down. I could picture him madly pacing to and fro in his office gazing at all the television monitors to confirm that what he is seeing is correct. It would be difficult for him to contain himself. He had already been waiting too long to see me submit, and I instinctively knew that he wanted to accompany the guards down to my cell so he can have the first shot to the back of my head.

He would be too cowardly to shoot me between the eyes I told myself to apply some black humour before my impending torture. He might start twitching and miss, which would make him appear like the fool he is in front of the psychopathic guards.

He had waited too long to achieve his level of authority and he was not going to belittle himself. I did, however, picture his hand shaking as he held and poised the gun. I almost laughed but could not because it would ruin my feigned submission.

I had purposely waited as long as I could before accepting my inevitable fate. It was the only amusing thing I could have in this black earthen dungeon. I was more amused at the thought that he was not going to shoot me and he would have to summon the interrogator commonly referred to in the administration of the Republic as the angel of death. This entertaining thought is what most psychologically prepared me for the pending round of abuse.

The guards arrived more maniacal than usual. I am more than certain that the warden had advised them to administer the most painful and dehumanizing form of torture at their disposal. He knew this would arouse them to exert the most extreme physical and psychological violation they were capable of conjuring in their merciless and emotionally bereft minds.

After force-feeding me unidentifiable food that closely resembled a blend of cockroach and scorpions, the jubilant guards unshackled me, placed a barely breathable orange sack over my head, and brusquely dragged me across the hall to the awaiting device. From the narrow slits covering my eyes, I could dimly discern a sarcophagus-like structure located in the middle of the room. As we moved farther into the chamber, I realized that they were guiding me to this tomb.

The casket was constructed out of red clay and had two folding doors that when opened revealed an abominable work of horror. The box was fitted with spikes that ran along the sides and adorned the insides of the doors. Each of the devices I had previously been subjected to defied my imagination, but this one surpassed them all. It was completely beyond any realm of reason why and how such a devise was ever manufactured. It was more astonishing that it continued to be used.

The tomb was cold, which ironically was a welcome reprieve from the suffocating desert heat. I never could comprehend how these thoughts went through my head. As the heavy doors closed over my naked body, the spikes pierced my exposed flesh from all directions, and I could feel the warm trickles of blood slowly exiting the punctured veins. When a long spike hit my bladder and kidneys I let out a yelp. It was the most excruciating pain ever to run through my body. When the spikes hit my eyes, I was happy that I had the sack over my head, or I am sure I would have been instantly blinded. The sharp points ensured that my eyes remained shut through the duration of the torture.

The device appeared to have been designed to provide the maximum degree of pain, discomfort, and mutilation that could last for weeks without killing its prisoner. The side spikes also could be lengthened and shortened by moving along the sockets. This functionality I discovered experientially when the guards increased the spike length to fully penetrate my arms, legs, belly, chest, shoulders, and buttocks.

Inside the chamber, I was completely pinned in and lacerated and surprisingly conscious. Throughout the entire process, I was acutely aware the physical injuries inflicted in this human tomb would kill me within a few days regardless of any interrogation. Writhing in numbing and constant pain, I knew that is exactly what the warden intended, but he once again would be mistaken. As usual, he did not give any credence to independent will and resolve probably because he had never exercised the sublime faculty himself.

Rarely had I.

When the guards finally removed me from my grave, my body was completely limp. The joints in my legs had me punctured, and my organs were slowly failing, and the constant pressure of the spikes on my eyes severely impaired my vision. The guards were like schoolchildren receiving a prize for good behaviour. The enjoyment they received from seeing me in my decrepit state made them almost giggle.

In an effort to prolong their amusement, rather than dragging or carrying me back as they had after the previous rounds of torture, they insisted on making me crawl back to my cell. The joints on my arms were barely attached, and my left shoulder was hanging off my body, and I still hadn't recovered from the contusions and numbness encountered in the earlier sessions.

I was lying on the floor. I knew I had to use my arm to prop myself up, but I lacked the physical strength. I could hear the guards cajoling and laughing. I had never felt so motivated and helpless. I wanted my solitude. I despised the murderous guards. Everything about them made me cringe. I could not believe that I had the audacity to sign their release papers and employ them at this corpse factory.

'Ugg!' I screamed in anguish at all my past mistakes and current predicament. It was no use. I could not clear my mind, and I could not move. I began to cry. Then I stopped. I would not and could not feel sorry for myself. I did not deserve it. If I were to cry, it should be for all the others, but they deserved more than tears.

I looked across the hall. Even with my blurred vision, it did not look so far. The taunting of the guards buzzed in my ears. Other than when I looked at myself in the mirror, I had never witnessed more detestable people than them. I needed to escape their presence. I just needed to think of how. I examined my situation and began to roll myself out of the death chamber toward my cell.

For an instant, the guards disappeared. I had cleared my mind of all external impediments and focussed solely on achieving my objective. *It would all be over soon,* I told myself with each roll. It was the last physical pain I would have to endure before entering the fire.

After what felt like hours, I felt the damp dark earth under my skin. *I made it,* I said, congratulating myself with a long sigh of relief. However, barely had I entered my cell when one of the guards slammed his pistol butt into my lacerated kidney while another knocked me over the head with a nightstick. The darting pain pinned me to my spot where I lay inert.

'Thought you were clever,' a guard mumbled.

'We will see how clever you feel in a few hours,' he said as he picked me up and re-shackled my ankles and wrists to the ceiling and floor posts. They all laughed then closed the door to return to report to the warden prior to returning to their leisurely activities.

I hung there working through the pain. I needed the spectacle to look like I was seriously considering giving up and accepting my instant death. I have never been with the warden watching the signs of life slowly drain from the prisoner's face. I don't think I could stomach it. I should have though because maybe it would have inspired me to act sooner.

I doubt it though.

I was too removed and blind with authority that I consciously chose only to fabricate bland speeches and blindly sign legislation instead of question it.

I call the warden a sycophant, and I patronize him for being a corporate climber and unthinkingly pursuing ambition and authority, but he was no different than I.

In some way, he was better. At least he dared to watch the process of death (albeit with perverse joy); I merely ignored it.

I could feel my body failing. I needed to be on the ground to stop the bleeding, minimize the pain, and perhaps even sleep. To get all that, I just had to stop thinking and allow the pain and feeling of helplessness come over me until I appear to be a corpse. It is only then that the warden will sound the alarm and initiate the interrogation process.

However, not thinking had become almost impossible since I had reinvigorated this innate human capacity a few months ago. It was a whole form of action and life itself that for twenty-eight years I had left dormant. It was if my entire past, present, and future collided into one; and I was face-to-face with the stranger that was myself.

The moment, I started thinking I wanted to examine everything so that I could understand and recognize the stranger. The process became addictive. I was losing sleep; I was walking into walls and forgetting to complete routine activities at work. Despite everything, I did not want to stop. For the first time in my life, I had felt happy and fulfilled—except for the haunting discoveries that I was a monster and I had played a major role destroying the world in the Republic.

For several months, I was sick to my stomach. Everywhere I went I saw destruction and nothingness. It was a living nightmare. I could not understand where all the people had gone. I felt alone and more and more insane. I needed someone to talk to, someone to acknowledge and respond to what I was thinking, but there were only zombies and myself.

For several months I had been thinking about ways to fix the situation, to find a way to stop the mounting insanity that was devouring my brain. Night and day, I would think and think and think. I am sure he saw me doing it. He loved to watch people and find a way to prey on their weaknesses. I am sure his alarm was raised, but he liked to bide his time. He enjoyed a good game. At the time, I was too absorbed to notice or to care.

One weekend, I was lying in bed waiting for the soccer match to commence on the television when I had a personal epiphany. I realized that the only way to stop thinking was to act. The moment I had this thought, my racing mind began to rest. It wasn't that I stopped thinking; but I was then able to direct my thinking into something tangible, concrete, and public. The insanity began to ebb because by acting, I was going to be able to place myself in the public to be seen and judged.

I viewed my planned action as an opportunity to start something new and a way to remember the deeds, words, people, and spirit of the past. The moment I planned to act is truly the first time that I felt free and alive. I could accept death because I was able to understand and participate in life.

Unfortunately the warden, guards, and interrogator—with all the weapons of torture, authority, and death behind them—did not understand. There was no amount of physical pain that could diminish this feeling. I was not afraid to die; I was only sad and disappointed that I had not experienced life long enough.

It was these thoughts that I desperately tried to clear from my mind to portray the look of death and persuade the expectant warden and guards to come. It was almost impossible. My mind kept reflecting upon everything I had done, everything that had happened, the history and tradition of the Republic, and what may be happening.

Most of all, my mind was contemplating my upcoming discussion with the interrogator. It would be a match of wits, concentration, patience, and will. Both of us desired the conversation, but neither of us would submit to the other's critical examination. It was going to be a crucial discussion that only he and I could have. The interview itself would not change anything or have an effect on the outside world, but it was an opportunity to finally talk face-to-face with the stranger in my head.

Stop thinking, I implored myself. *You know he can see everything and will not believe you have quit. It is not a time for thinking but a time for action.* This statement ended up being the perfect dose of reality. Shortly afterward, my mind began to ease, and I could let the back-and-forth flicker in my eyes abate and become catatonic and helpless. *Remain still for hours. Be abject. Wait.*

The hours passed on. Nothing. He was officious and did not want to raise a false alarm. He had to be sure that I no longer held on to his conception of life. Without moving, I was beginning to wonder how long he would be scrutinizing the screens. I began to think that he may have finally fallen asleep, but that was not likely.

He was watching me, waiting to see if I truly cracked. He was intelligent enough to know that I had little patience, and with prolonged waiting, he would win the mental battle. Not this one; I was too determined. *Stare fixedly. Don't think or move. Time moved slowly. Concentrate and let the hours go by.*

Ringgggg! The sound of the alarm almost made me jump out of skin. I had managed to enter into a sleep-like state to maintain my abject appearance that any noise was a jolt to my slumbering consciousness. I had to control every remaining sinew of my body not to move and appear to be startled, alert, and caring.

In all my mental coaxing to put on the façade of death, I had forgotten to remember to retain my composure when the blare of the alarm went off. I was hoping that he did not see my fists and jaw clench. If he had all of my plans would be over. He would order the anxiously awaiting guards to take me back to the iron maiden and bled to death before I could make it back to the cell.

Fortunately my composure worked. A short while after the alarm sounded, I could hear the rhythmic thumping of the army-issue boots echoing through the empty building down the winding stone staircase and the darkened hallway toward my cell, then the tambourine jingle of keys, the entry of metal into a slot, turn, pop, creak, and then silence.

Click tap! Click tap! Click tap came the sound of the warden's cheap patent leather shoes leaving the cement floors of the hallway onto the earthen floor of the cell. I don't think he had ever been down here before because in the space between the hall and the cell, I could see him hesitate.

The cell was more vile and putrid than he could view from the sterile confines of his pristine office. I could see him wretch and turn away. In response to his rookie reaction, a crescendo of snickers could be heard from the guards.

'Silence,' he said after spewing a volley of vomit onto the floor.

'Clean this up and hand me a mask.'

The light illuminating from his headlamp indicated that he was kneeling on the ground. I could hear him chocking, trying in vain to hold back another eruption of vomit.

The sound and sight of someone vomiting always incited my gag reflex. The continued dry heaving, puking, and its rancid smell affected me more than the sound of the alarm. Fortunately all attention was focussed on the warden, and I could move my head to fight back my overwhelming urge to puke. I was most concerned about choking myself to death trying to keep it in. His continued spells were almost pushing me beyond my greatest resolve.

Finally it was over. I held my breath and madly counted to ten in my head over and over again to regain my concentration. A guard returned with a mop and steal bucket and began cleaning up the mess. The warden took deep breaths and allowed himself to recover.

The smell in the cell was absolutely nauseating. There was urine, blood, and fecal matter forming the base of the cell. Any virgin nose would have evoked the same response experienced by the warden. When I first arrived, I was too cooked to respond to any stimulus and had gradually acclimatized myself to the putrid surroundings.

The smell was unlikely to affect the guards due to the nature of their earlier careers—stalking, trapping and torturing, mutilating, and doing post-mortem organ extraction. Thus, when the warden gagged their natural instinct to torment their victims their desire to inflict life-threatening harm was intensified. The compliance of the guards to listen to the weak warden rested entirely on their ability to engage in continuous torture and mutilation with each transported prisoner.

The most disturbing premise about the administration of prison 535 was the need to have perpetual prisoners. The prison had been virtually transformed into an assembly line death camp. Almost every week, a new prisoner needed to be supplied to keep the guards happy. If too much time elapsed, it was understood in the formation meetings, the guards would begin to get anxious and bored and would turn to the warden.

Once the warden was dead, the guards would then emigrate into the cities and towns and go on a mass killing spree, thereby disrupting the order of the Republic. Thus, to appease the guards, a new political prisoner was brought to the prison for the pleasure of the guards like mice being fed to a large snake. In turn, the citizens of the Republic felt more secure, and the administration maintained its authority.

In devising the plans, no one had had the foresight of the eventual annihilation of every person residing in the Republic, except for the interrogator. Most believed it was a necessary establishment to contain terrorism and work to restore peace and security to the beleaguered Republic. I, of course, did not think about this either until recently— much too late for the millions murdered here before me.

As I was having this thought, the warden had sufficiently recovered and resumed his click-clack into the cell. Through the glare of the headlamp ridiculously strapped around his halfbald head, I could see the square white face mask tightly tied over his nose and mouth. It took my remaining composure not to laugh and continue to stare blankly ahead.

For approximately a millisecond upon looking at him, I felt a slight affinity to the guard's uncontrollable snickering. It was true. In the advent of a dry spell of prisoners, they would devour him.

The warden looked at me with absolute mirth in his beady little eyes. I remained steadfast. He pushed me, punched me, and had a guard remove my right eye with his cold and dull bowie knife to ensure that I was not faking. Through the pain of the cold steel knife digging into my eye socket and removing my eye, I did not flinch. I had already experienced so much physical pain that I think I had become impervious to it.

My continued inertia was successful assuring him of my complacence. When my eye was being removed, I noticed him cringe before he exerted a large grin. It was the look of a lottery winner. He thought he had finally managed to defeat his nemesis. For the first time in his life, I was under his complete authority. The entire experience was almost too much for him to bear. When the eye was out, he practically jumped on top of me in a hasty effort to remove my bonds and see me crumble to the floor.

In his haste to shoot me, the warden accidentally knocked the guard who had paused to admire his prize of my eye before depositing it into his shirt pocket to eat later. In reaction to the unexpected hit, the guard stumbled causing my eye to fly into the black air. In entirely different circumstance, the spectacle could be construed as comical.

Intent on regaining his prize, the guard pushed the embarrassed warden aside into the toilet dugout causing him to land in a pile of undecomposed feces. His entire buttocks, back, and head were covered in slimy black shit, which caused him to let out a muffled scream under his mask. Undeterred by his insubordinate action, the disturbed guard ignored the warden, caught the airborne eye, and exited the cell to rejoin his mates. Throughout the farce, I remained transfixed. The desire to have the ordeal over enabled me to retain my corpselike composure.

Regaining his composure, the warden stepped out of the toilet and resumed his approach toward me. This time, he was more cautious and deliberate. He had the countenance of servility that a person displays upon being belittled in front of someone considered superior. He walked slowly staring at me directly in the face in an effort to reassert his mastery. I obliged and did not blink. He stood still for a long moment and then removed the shackle keys from his grey pant pocket and removed my bound limps one at a time.

When the last chain was removed from my limp wrist, my body crumbled to the ground. Like every previous prisoner, I remained motionless in a fatal position until I was addressed by an officer or, in my special case, the warden. Stepping up, he crouched down beside my exposed ear and clearly and proudly instructed me to state interrogation if I desired an interrogation or to move a part of my stationary body to receive an immediate death by firing squad. I purposely did not react to the instruction.

190 WHERE ARE THE HEROES?

My unresponsiveness outwardly annoyed him. He cleared his throat and repeated the instruction in a louder and more demanding tone. I hesitated then, without moving meekly, replied, 'Interrogation please.'

I could hear the poised gun drop out of his hand and land on the packed earth. His breathing had increased, and I could feel his close body twitching. For a while, he was silent; then he repeated the instruction the third time. When he finished, I shouted as loudly as I could, 'INTERROGATION PLEASE!' so there would no longer be any misunderstanding.

Upon hearing me speak, the warden jumped up and began agitatedly pacing back and forth. I could also hear the guards getting restless. They had never had to wait this long before an execution, and they were getting impatient for the thrill of the kill. In the passing moments, I could tell that he was contemplating shooting me anyway, but he knew he could not. The cell's video and audio system were connected to the Department of Internal Republic Security, which dutifully recorded everything.

The warden was deeply distressed. He could not stop pacing and ignored his personal peril screaming at the guards to return to their quarters. The animal-like shriek from the warden's mouth stunned the vicious guards who uncharacteristically immediately obeyed him and left the hallway. Then it was just he and I.

I. lying on the wet dark fecal ground and he widely pointing the gun at me threatening to shoot while simultaneously wailing and cursing me for ruining his entire career.

I said nothing—mostly because I had taken too much energy to say interrogation. Also, his relentless agitation stated to have an unsettling effect upon me. There were several times that I thought he would just shoot me and maybe shoot himself. He was afraid of the interrogator and did not want him to come to the prison. He perceived the whole episode as defeat and a possible demotion. Fearing his irrational reprisal, I decided to remain inert until his little sanity returned.

The interrogator was a handsome tall man with a kind smile in his mid-forties. He was highly intelligent, cultured, and always seemed to be in a good mood. He whistled and cheerfully said hello to everyone he passed. His presence was so unassuming that when one first met him, they felt a pause from the madness, agony, and death that pervaded the alter days of the Republic.

When he attended administrative meetings, his suits were always impeccably tailored, cleaned, and pressed. When discussing policy, he preferred to watch and listen to the arguments with an air of cursory interest to the legislation that was being drafted before him, legislation of which he was the primary architect. Lastly, regardless of his perfect physical health, he always carried a gold can with a disturbing skull as its knob. He did so because he liked its style but more so because it was a convenient pointer for instructing people where to go, which for some reason people unhesitatingly obeyed.

His outward arrogance is tempered by his charm, wit, and aura of mystery. He was not a man that anyone would initially believe to be the architect and sometime perpetrator of such heinous and diabolical acts of horror and terror ever known in the history of man.

No one considered him to be the sinister or diabolical person because they were too smitten by the thick veneer of his charm and wit. It was only when one has the opportunity to have a genuine conversation with him that one is able to discern his true opinion of humanity and that one can get a glimpse into the monster that he really was.

When one was privy to such an encounter, all the charm carried in his outward demeanour immediately dissipated into the cold and chilly air that he left in his wake. When this visual transformation occurred, the only thing visible in his visage was the cold, calculating, joyful, and trifling manner in which he snuffed out the life of an animal or a person.

In such a conversation, he would readily admit that he was able to issue an edict to annihilate a person or a group of people because he *despises all members of the human race*. He may have also shared his fascination with nothingness and that presiding over life and death gave him the greatest feeling of inner pleasure. I had been privy to this discussion that left my body to run cold. Seeing him again was not something I looked forward to. However, besides being aware that he is a cold, ruthless killer, I know his most inner secret. He is bored. His boredom is what would make him anxious to speak to me. He was probably on the military chopper right now flying at top speed to get here.

The warden was afraid of him, so he did not shoot me. Instead he stopped yelling, returned the gun to its holster, and dejectedly left the prison cell. A while later, he returned with a few guards to assist me to the shower where I was washed, bandaged, and clothed. I was then carried to another cell equipped with a bench, bed, toilet, and window.

As soon as I entered my new haven I lay down on the hard mattress and slept until I was awakened by the loud roar of his chopper rumbled to a halt in the courtyard of the prison. I had been in a deep slumber and easily startled. For a moment, I forgot where I was or what was happening because it was the first real sleep I had had since my arrival. I felt very groggy and had difficulty opening my eye. My body was greedy and did not want the rest to terminate.

However, although I desperately wanted to return to sleep, I wanted my mind to be alert. It usually takes me a good two hours before I function after sleeping; time, I knew that I did not have. My severed joints prevented me from sitting myself up in the hard mattress, so I had to attempt to remain awake in my slumbering position.

The light coming through the barred window from the blaring desert sun was blinding. My single eye had become unaccustomed to light after being confined in darkness for what felt like eternity. Now that I was awake, I did not think it would be possible to return to sleep until the burning sun went down. All I could do was rest and think before the guards arrived to escort me to the interrogation room.

Fortunately I did not have to wait too long. The interrogator was no doubt eager to get the process started and was impatiently waiting in the interrogation room. Within minutes of the chopper landing, the warden followed by two guards opened my cell to drag me to the interrogation room.

The room was small. There were no windows, and the only light came from a single exposed yellow light bulb hanging over the table in the middle of the room. The table was rectangular with two chairs facing directly across each other. There was nothing on the table or other obstacles in the room. It was just the handsome interrogator and I.

When we entered the room, he was already sitting. His gold cane with the skull knob was resting on the table with the sharp tip pointing directly at the chair I was to occupy. To emphasize his intention, he nudged the cane forward indicating to the guard carrying me to place me there.

The chair was made of dark mahogany cushioned by paisley embroidery and sported two thick armrests. In my deformed and mutilated physical condition, I was surprisingly comfortable.

After the guard had dutifully placed me in the chair, the interrogator pushed the cane tip toward the door indicating the guards and warden to exit. When the heavy wooden door closed, I marvelled at the ability the interrogator had in even charming and controlling the psychopathic guards. He truly had demonic qualities. In this surreal world, he was the master of all—well, almost all.

While I was engaging in this thought process, the interrogator had repositioned the can's tip to point directly to my heart and stared at me with his most charming and welcoming smile. When I had released myself from my thoughts, he put his long elegant hands on the table and looked me directly in the eye and nodded to indicate that the interrogation was ready to begin. I nodded back in consent and felt my pulse race and my hands become clammy at the long-awaited opportunity for dialogue.

'Welcome to the interrogation,' he said.

'I have been expecting you for a while. You are a fascinating specimen. I could have trapped you long ago, but I was curious to see what you were planning to do and what effect it might have.'

I continued to watch and listen.

'On behalf of the Republic,' he continued undeterred by my silence, and your request, I am here to grant you this interrogation. This discussion will be the last one you will have before I send you alive into the hot glowing flames of the furnace to die.'

He smiled.

'I don't need to remind you,' he continued, that this is not a trial. You are guilty and have already been sentenced to death. Everything you say is meaningless. It will not be recorded, and it will not be remembered. Do you understand?'

I said I understand.

'Good,' he replied.

'As you know, boredom has always plagued me. It brings me a modicum of amusement to share this last conversation with you.'

He picked up the cane and tapped me on the shoulder, the returned it to the table in its original position.

'So I shall begin.'

I nodded in consent.

'Excellent,' he responded with a wide grin. 'Let us begin.'

Without further expression, he efficiently launched into the interrogation.

That was a fine stunt you pulled setting up a hacker-proof Web site containing all the names of the people exterminated since the implementation of the DNA-badge legislation along with a highlighted copy of the constitution. Do you actually think that people would be interested in reading your pathetic pamphlets detailing the origin of the terrorist attacks and would go to the site for more information?

'I have faith in human curiosity and the search for truth.'

The truth is that you are an identified terrorist that has been arrested for crimes against the safety of the Republic. Do you think anyone will believe what you have written?

I don't know if they will believe it, as you say. It does seem rather incredulous, but I do think that they will read it and maybe attempt to find out if it is true. If they don't, I know that I have done my best to restore the remembrance of all the people who were killed into the history of the Republic.

After this response, he paused, shrugged his broad shoulders, then looked at me with his steel-cold, soul-delving stare before resuming the interrogation.

You are a sorry-looking individual. How have you enjoyed your stay at these fine quarters that you have judiciously reopened?

I smiled. I have been housed in the most distinguished quarters for someone of my disposition. I have had regular visits and the best food available in these arid parts. I cannot say that it has been entirely enjoyable, but it has been a nice retreat to think and recollect myself. It was also a great reprieve from the constant exigencies of work.

I paused.

As far as judiciously reopening this place, I vehemently disagree. It was one of the most reprehensible acts committed by me during my tenure as the minister of the Department of Internal Republic Security. The establishment itself has done absolutely nothing to reduce the number of people being identified as terrorists and has not made the streets any safer.

Furthermore, as far as signing the release of the psychopaths from their solitary cells to become prison guards is concerned, nothing could me more unjust than that. It is like releasing an incurable plague upon the world that will work its venom through every available person there is left to destroy. This conception of justice I do not share. I agree that it is justice that I should die, and even more just that I should die in the confines of my own doing, but it is not just. Nothing thoughtless can ever be considered just.

Since you seem to be so learned, why don't you edify me on your newly contrived conception of justice?

As you wish, although you are most likely incapable of comprehending it. Justice is the ability to appear and be seen by others. This prison is the exact antithesis of justice. It hides people. It takes them into the most remote and desolate part of the Republic where plants and animals cannot even survive. It places them in isolation, and it slowly kills them powerless and alone. There is no recognition and no remembrance. It is not justice; it is a crime. Not only is it a crime, it is the most heinous crime imaginable. It is a crime against humanity, as far worse crime than the one I am charged with as a crime against the Republic.'

That explanation only demonstrates how insane you are. If only the sterilization practices had more time to have been implemented, then it is possible that your defective genes would not have propagated. Justice is the law. You know the law because you wrote it. The law condemns any act of public protest as an open and deliberate act to promote terrorism and is punishable by death. Do you not agree, or has your feeble mind moved beyond the limits of reality?

Yes, I agree that that what you said is the law, but I disagree that I am insane. This is the most sane I have ever been. It is you who is mad. But this is not the time or place to exchange personal insults. It will not do either of us any good. I will do my best to stick to answering your questions.

'I thought this may seem equally as insane to you, I posit that the law is not always just; and when an unjust law is legislated, it is the responsibility of the populace to stand up against it. A law can only be just if it enables its subjects to interact freely with each other in public and promotes protests so that all views can be heard. Thus, it logically follows that a law that limits human interaction, prohibits protests, and promotes fear and death can never be just.

Tell me, my little traitor, were your last actions intended to overthrow the democratically elected government of the Republic?

'Yes, that was my intention.'

Did you not participate in the creation of laws to prevent terrorism and protect citizens from the ever-present threat of terrorists such as yourself?

Yes, I did participate in the creation of the antiterrorist laws, but I do not believe that they protected the citizens. Quite the contrary, I believe that they created an entire department of terrorists who had legislative authority to host a reign of terror over the very citizens they were created to protect.

And did you prohibit all court review and considered it necessary to prohibit court review of people who had not committed any crimes but who, you thought, might possibly commit a crime?

'Yes, I drafted legislation to have people arrested and killed who had not yet committed any crime.'

And did you enact these policies in full knowledge that the terrorist threat was manufactured as a way for the chancellor magistrate to retain his position and implement his vision of the Republic?

'Yes, I did.'

Thank you. And were you not willing turn a blind eye to the fate of the immigrants—even your friends, lover, and neighbours—knowing that the legislation would result in their segregation, disappearance, and eventual death?

My mouth was dry. I could not reply. All I could do was nod in assent. My silent agreement was not satisfactory to him, so he urged me to reply louder. This encouragement was unsettling. I knew that I did, but for some reason, I did not want to say it out loud.

I had not anticipated this act of feebleness. For some reason, I did not want to verbally respond to the question. Instead I wanted to remain mute and deny the sitting witness verbal testimony to my transgressions.

My silence almost made him giddy. This irritated me more, but still I could not respond. I was a contender on the rope, exposed and unable to defend myself. With each blow, my will failed a bit more. My dumbness only reconfirmed my weakness. He was correct. I had betrayed my friends, lover, and neighbours through my silence and complicity and, even worse, through the policies I helped to enact. I knew that the chancellor magistrate hated the immigrants and had been planning for years to eliminate them.

I knew that he blamed all the economic and social difficulties experienced in the Republic on the immigrants. He despised them because they always had a ready access to money and never seemed to be unemployed. He hated them because they appeared to do better in school and had different skin colour that would one day mix and 'taint the pure colour of the Republic.' I knew all of this because he told me. I knew all of this, and I enacted the policies to eliminate them. I suddenly felt sick and wanted to collapse as the question of my complicity loomed over my head tight as a noose.

I moved my lips, but no words came out. I am guilty, but why could I not admit it?

Sorry, I can't hear you he interjected. You will have to speak louder.

The sound of a voice made me jump out of my skin. I had been lost in the silence that the sound of another voice reverted through my head, almost knocking a fatal blow to my reeling inner self.

He frowned and looked at his watch in dismay. I know he expected more, but I was a helpless impostor. I thought I had examined myself and was ready for the fight. The problem was that I had not been examined by others and had never had to verbally admit my guilt, my crime to humanity.

He was becoming impatient.

Can you answer the question or not? He scoffed. If not, let us stop this charade and end this interrogation. He then picked up his cane and motioned to summon the warden.

'NO!' I screamed, surprising the vice chancellor magistrate and myself by the sound of its shrill terror. 'I can answer the question,' I pleaded.

He sat back down.

'Yes,' I said.

What?

'Yes,' I repeated.

He looked amused. I was deflated but decidedly relieved. It was as if a huge burden had been lifted from my shoulders. I had finally confessed my guilt and had lifted myself off the rope to continue the gladiatorial fight unto death.

So why, may I ask, my once faithful ally, after saving the Republic from being destroyed by the pestilence of cultural diversity and racial mixing did you decide to openly oppose the laws you arduously helped to enact and actively promote and engage in subterfuge?

'I realized that I had become a murderer and had encouraged others to become one too. Day after day, I saw and authorized disappearances and killings in the name of protecting the sanctity of the Republic, and I could no longer live with myself.'

Please don't tell me that you have suddenly developed a conscience and want to repent for all your sins. You and I both know that the time for heroes has long passed.

A hero is a person of distinguished valour or enterprise in danger or fortitude in suffering hence a person regarded as possessing noble qualities. I am far from possessing any of these characteristics. A hero fights for justice, not opposes it; and lastly, a hero is also someone who stands up and fights when the chips are down. This I did not do and have not done. All I did was look in the mirror one day and saw what a monster I had become and what a mockery the Republic had become.

I am here because I know I did not want to use my thoughtlessness as a shield anymore. I wanted to be able to look myself in the mirror and be able to know and appreciate the person who was looking back at me. When I first looked in the mirror, I saw what I am seeing across the table from me now. I saw an intelligent, witty, charming, and good-looking person who was capable of committing the most heinous acts without a second thought. That vision shocked and haunted me in every reflective object that I passed until it seeped into my head and became a part of my consciousness.

That person sneered, smiled, and hummed its way through every antiterrorist policy implementation. That person turned away at the pleading cries from the immigrants as they were shot to death. That person ignored the disappearance of neighbours, friends, and family until there was no one else to see. Every day and night, I struggled to figure out whom that person in the reflection was until I realized that it was myself. I was that monster in the mirror.

After realizing this frightful discovery, I screamed and screamed and screamed until I had no energy left, then I collapsed onto the cold ceramic tiles on my bathroom floor, and wept. I wept for all my stupidity, and I wept for all the people I had legislated to kill. I realized that I was an active and willing accessory to all the external madness. In that moment of lucidity, I pledged myself that I would do something before everything and everyone was dead and forgotten.

My response agitated him a little; he began playing with his cane, rolling it over and over on his palm as he contemplated my response. After a short spell of silence, he responded.

You are correct. We are the same. However, neither of us has killed anyone. Your little conscience friend has led you astray. All we have done is try to make the Republic a safer and terrorist-free nation. The guards kill the prisoners; the military kill the terrorists, and the people kill each other. We have merely been innocent bystanders in a crusade for peace and security. You forget that people don't want freedom; they want security, stability, and to be left alone. We just provide the structure for that. I, however, will make one exception. I will incinerate you at the close of this interrogation.

While it is true that you and I have never literally killed anyone, our policies and silence have amounted to a veritable genocide. The policies made the guns, and the silence pulled the trigger. That is where I will end our similarity. I am guilty of murder because I did not stop to think about the repercussions of the legislation or my actions. I quietly went thorough life without managing to reflect on a single thing.

The greatest murder is the thoughtless murder because it is the one that no one can explain or prove. The level of my shallowness and thoughtlessness was pathological. It is irrational to stand aside and watch everyone disappear. It is irrational to implement a policy that eradicated one-fourth of the population with the swoop of a pen.

People have been killing one other because they live in absolute terror. When the legislation was first passed, there were several pockets of resistance, which were systematically exterminated by the very mechanisms and units that were created to protect them. In the wake of the mass slaughters and purges, terror appeared to be spreading on the surface of the Republic like a fungus.

The real evil was not the people killing other people, but the administration fostering a regime of fear and terror that could only result in complete annihilation of every resident. Thus, the greatest crime was the lack of judgement exercised by us all to stop the terror and killings from happening—to ignore the unjust policies of the government instead of implementing them and accepting them as law.

Be that as it may, why are you willing to risk your life for a group of people who had long given up on the notion of life when you could have passed through life untouched?

That is a good question. I did not consider my actions a risk to my life because everything around me was already dead. I regarded it as a way to be alive. It was a way to start something new to obviate the mad march into oblivion. In my thinking, I realized that things did not have to continue relentless along the same pathological trajectory. All that was required was for someone to do something new and unexpected, and that is what I did. The solution was so simple. I just had to devise a plan and carry it out, and that is exactly what I did.

But you knew that you were going to die and that your actions and your subsequent death would be meaningless, so why did you bother?

I bothered because my conscience compelled me to act. While at work, walking home, on the public transit, riding my bicycle, or in a shopping mall, I saw looks of anguish and desire for something new on the sullen faces of many people.

I understood that the fear rendered most people silent, but in the eyes of the citizens, I also saw a window of willingness to spontaneously act and shake off the invisible bonds imposed by the constant reign of terror if the circumstances presented themselves.

In those lonely and dejected faces, I saw the possibility for a deluge of change—change that would make people like you to be afraid because the monstrous world that you built would disappear, and it was uncomfortable for you to go on living with your diabolical self.

Even if this change did not occur, I had long ago decided that if no movement for change occurred as a result of my actions, at least I had tried and could be at peace with my constant internal inquisitor who asks me if I feel ashamed at letting the people kill and disappear from the world we live in.

Even if your little stunt succeeded and some onlookers listened, read, and began to think about what you were saying, what makes you think they would have any power to stop the killing and disappearances?

I know that if there would be a group of people who spontaneously gather together to stop the killings, false arrests, and disappearances, they would have more power than any weapon created.

Hum. How intriguing. What makes you think that?

I know that they would have the power to stop the senseless killings because the inherent nature of power is non-violent.

Now I know you have sustained massive brain injury in your tenure here. How can power possibly be non-violent when it has the ability to stop or destroy?

It is non-violent because only violence can destroy power. As you are well aware, decreases in power, such as the enactment of the DNA database and the immigration policy, openly invites violence. Violence is a substitute for power. It is not and should never be confused with power. There is a reason why the founders of the Republic devised a government structure that instituted the rule of law that rested on the power of the people to put an end to arbitrary rule and oppression of one over the many.

The drafters of the constitution properly understood the notion of power as non-violent. They understood that power requires a number of people whereas violence merely requires an instrument of death rather than people to carry out its desired end. Power itself occurs as soon as people come together. It is exercised when those people act together to achieve a desired end. I think that you understand this and are afraid of the strength of power, and you are afraid because it is people acting and being together for a common cause—something you despise.

The common thread in all the post power plant explosions was to limit the social interactions between people and empty the once-populated streets. The legislation would have done this if you and the chancellor magistrate did not understand and fear power. Both of you clearly understood that terror, established by violence, can destroy power. The terror turns people not only against their unknown enemies but also their friends and family until all form or possibility of power has been eliminated. Thus, in sum, power and violence are diametrically opposing forces.

Well, that was an interesting, if not entirely naive, speech. How do you propose that these people are going to come together and act when you know that the administration monitors all telecommunications and cyber conversations and would arrest each of them for crimes against the Republic?

First of all, these people would have to have read the material or listened to my interrupted public speech. Then they would have engaged in an internal dialogue with themselves to comprehend the material and judge whether it is worthwhile acting and sharing with each other or not. This activity would have to be done in solitude and kept private to avoid detection until the individual felt confident or compelled enough to discuss the material with someone else. I have discovered that conversations do not have to occur over the telephone or the Internet. They will most likely begin with themselves in the form of a dialogue and then spread to a person until there is a critical mass and the beginning of the reassertion of the public space.

How would these congregating people be able to use their power to stop any law-abiding citizen from reporting any suspicious or untoward behaviour of individuals to the terrorist-prevention hotline, which would also result their arrest and disappearance as you say?

A simple answer to this question is that they would not be able to prevent this from occurring. However, I posit that if a large group of people were to gather together to participate in a conversation or an activity, the so-called law-abiding citizen would most likely move closer to the group to find out what is going on. This citizen would most likely refrain from calling because he or she had joined the group or because it's a lot more difficult to report and arrest a large group than it is to report and arrest an individual.

Even if these people would be able to gather together to act and speak with each other in a public space without the reprisal of being arrested, which I highly doubt would occur, what makes you feel confident that they would act to prevent further arrests and other killings?

If these people can actually get to the point where they have formed a large group and are willing to act and speak together, they have already stopped some arrests and some killings. Through their speaking and acting, these people would be re-entering the public space of human interaction that ensures that others are always present to share, discourse, and act with. It is the opposite of creating corpses that the present regime so reveres.

Regardless of everything that you have just said, do you not think the whole thing is moot? Everyone has too much fear to talk to another person, let alone form a group.

I agree that there is a great deal of fear in the Republic, but fear can be overcome. It is up to each individual person to judge and decide to leave the shadows of loneliness and enter the public space of the Republic. Personally I think that perpetual loneliness is a far more fearsome prospect than taking a risk to talk to another person and perhaps gather together in a public space. In all, however, I would not have been nearly as confident in my actions if I had witnessed anxiety rather than fear in the actions and words of the remaining citizens.

That is an absurd statement. Why is anxiety a worse feeling than fear?

Fear is an emotion that is triggered by a threat. In a number of cases, as we have seen over the past few years, fear can be quite debilitating and cause one to freeze or to cease one's actions. However, fear is something that can be overcome and lead one to act again once the threat is removed.

Anxiety, on the other hand, is an emotion directly related to the impossibility of attaining a desired end. Unlike fear, intense feelings of anxiety do not go away. It is something that continually makes us feel ill at ease in every situation. It is an emotion that at once can rob a person of speech and eliminate all possibility of action. It is the one emotion that makes one run away, hide, and disappear from oneself and the world. Fear can resemble anxiety, but it is not the same.

What makes you think the prospect of torture and death for the majority of people reading your antiquated pamphlets or listening to your pathetic broadcast would not evoke paralysing anxiety into the hearts and minds of your expected heroes?

All I can say in response to that presumptive question is that I am here; and as you know, where there is one cockroach as you say, there is most likely another. You and I know that no further change of laws, policies, or amount of torture can prevent people from taking a risk. That is what being human is all about.

Be honest with yourself. In a choice of life or death, do you think any sane person would choose death? I have seen it too many times. The human will to live is a very powerful instrument.

In an absolute option to choose to live or to die, I would agree with you. However, in a situation when one is already dead, anxiety over dying disappears in the possibility of gaining an opportunity to live.

What are you talking about?

I apologize for being cryptic. I will do my best to further elucidate this vital concept to you.

In a situation similar to the current condition of the Republic, one is acutely aware of death and is constantly struggling to find a way to live.

To truly live, one understands that one must have the ability to live and interact with others on a regular basis. When this opportunity disappears or fades away, so too does life; and one begins to take on the face of death.

Thus, in the absence of a space to speak and interact with one's peers, death has already prevailed over life leaving the door open for people to eschew their original apprehension toward death in an attempt to re-establish life. In the attempt to re-establish life, the threat of death is not possible because one is already dead. Consequently, the only viable option to triumph over death is to rebuild the world—the only place that cultivates and nurtures life. This pursuit will occur until either the world is re-established or every living person has been killed. Contrary to your sadistic intentions, the threat of death and torture are meaningless in the wake of human will.'

Do you actually think that your literature will inspire people to live? After all, as you said, they have already taken on the face of death.

The purpose of my action and the literature I distributed was to remind people of history. In this regard, I hope that they are inspired to remember. But remembering is not acting. It is merely recounting an earlier event. The desire to live has to come from the people themselves. If it does, then there can be history and remembrance because there will be action and a story to tell. The desire to act and, thus, put history into motion arises from the realization that a person is not alone. It is a realization that there are others, and because there are others, there is the possibility of freedom and life. However, the realization of others is not enough; the only thing that can move someone to act in the face of death is a genuine feeling of personal responsibility.

'*How does personal responsibility motivate one to act?*'

Personal responsibility motivates a person to act by considering the well-being of others. It is the understanding that my actions affect the lives of others. Thus, it informs each person that something must be done to preserve the welfare of others. Taking this notion further, knowing that everyone benefits from the existence of a shared public space compels the individual to overcome fear by stepping into the world for the purpose of speaking, being, and acting with others. By doing so, the public space is re-established, and human interaction and freedom can recommence.

That is, without a doubt, the most idealist statement I have ever heard. If I thought someone cared, I might even give it some thought, but life as an ideal is dead. Isn't life meaningless? So what is there to remember? We are born. We live, and we die. What did we really leave behind but a grave with a useless name?

Obviously if I shared your vision, I would not be sitting here. I may have been a coward and a willing participant in your murderous scheme to create and collect corpses, but I never did ever think or contemplate the idea that life is meaningless and should, therefore, be snuffed out. In fact, I have always considered life to be precious and worth fighting or dying for. I also do not believe that anyone else agrees with you, not even your friend, the chancellor magistrate. I agree that people have been slumbering in the hurricane of terror, but they have not given up nor will ever be on the essence of life.

Life itself holds meaning and can only become meaningless in the absence of people. As long as there are people, there is always the possibility of action, which—when witnessed—becomes a story to be told and retold in history. History is nothing other than the story of human action. In that story, each person has the ability to be a main character to be recorded and remembered forever. However, the story—to be told—requires the supporting cast of every other person and a name.

I compiled the list of names of every person killed since the explosion of the power plant and distributed it in the park so that history could live on and those innocent people could have meaning and be remembered. A name is all we have to mark our place in the world, but the world is required for a mark to be made. Thus, a name is needed to preserve history, and for history to exist, there must be a space in the world for people to act and speak to create the story. It is for the possible reinvigoration of history and a space in the world that I chose to stand up in public, willing to embrace the sceptre of death that awaited me.

Clap, clap, clap. 'Bravo,' he said.

That was a fine speech. It is truly worthy of a reward of which I am more than happy to oblige. Because you so reverently adore life, I am going to give you the special privilege of cremating you alive. That way, you will be able to feel all the meaningful intensity of your life burning out of your body as you scream yourself to death.

I remained nonplused. Throughout the incarceration, my physical life had been drained out of me. I had had my interrogation and was ready to die. How and when this occurred was of no concern.

He then recollected himself and presented his eulogy to me.

I was hoping our discussion would break or at least crack the surreal walls that he housed himself in, but it did not. He enjoyed the nightmare and wanted everyone else to as well—anyone that did not became an instant statistic to the already-high body count. It was at that moment that I realized he could not think because he too was already dead. He was the sire of the living dead, and I was a disappointing progeny.

I cannot emphasize how disappointed I am with you. You were my best student, and now I have to kill you. It was a pleasure to be able to speak to someone as intelligent. It is something I am going to miss. I thought you understood me, but, alas, I was wrong.

He sighed and shook his head sadly before looking directly at me with his narrow cold grey eyes.

It behoves me not to have the authority to forgive and pardon you for your treachery and betrayal, but you broke the law, and the law must be obeyed. As the constitution states, it is higher than you or I. We are all its subjects.

Putting on his most charming face, he then leaned across the table to put his hand on my shoulder and whispered: 'Don't worry. I remember everyone I kill.'

He then slid back into his chair, smiled his usual unassuming grin, and menacingly toyed with the skull on the head of his cane looking at me until he got bored again and decided to push the button to indicate to the warden that the discussion was over.

Immediately after he buzzed the door to be opened, the warden—accompanied with the same two guards—entered the room. When he entered the room, the warden glared at me before glancing at the interrogator for approval.

With his usual gaiety, the vice chancellor magistrate gave him the patronizing nod of his head and then absently pointed his cane to the door to indicate that the interrogation was over and it was time to for everyone to leave. The two guards and the warden took the cue and proceeded to pick me up and carry me down the long empty aisle of cells until reaching my appointed cage where I was deposited on the bed with the computer to wait for the flames in the incinerator to be rekindled.

EPILOGUE

I don't feel well. One minute I am burning hot, and the next I am freezing futilely searching for a blanket to cover and warm my aching and shivering body. At all times my hands are cold, clammy, and shaking. I stop typing to clench them in a fist in a vain attempt to steady them, but it is to no avail. *There isn't much time left, and I must press on.*

After sitting in 535 for at least a week, I sense there is definitely something different about today. It is not something I can pinpoint; it is just a nagging feeling that almost encourages me to stop writing and return to my more natural state of contemplation. The arid air around my barren cell is restless—a small warning that my time is approaching its end.

My teeth are now chattering, and every movement sends a fresh burst of aches through my decaying body. My eye strains to focus in the blur of the pale dawn desert light. It too is sore. The fever is enveloping me. I am beginning to become disoriented. The urge for sleep and silence overwhelms me. I feel nauseous. I attempt to vomit, but my empty stomach brings forth nothing but another spasm of pain and uncontrollable shivering.

I am clinging onto the small computer for life support. I cannot rest until I finish my objective. I must find my encrypted Web site and paste all the names of the people who have disappeared and been murdered since the promulgation of the DNA-badge legislation. Everything is spinning. I am now uncertain between reality and fantasy. My eye draws back into my pounding head as I stare at the streaming news story on the computer.

The chancellor magistrate has been shot and killed by the head of the armed forces. With the absence of the vice chancellor magistrate, the Republic is in chaos. Civilians have stormed the administration offices routing the files and attacking the employees. Others have joined the military rebels. Few support the Internal Republic Security forces, but they have control over the majority of the Republic and access to the arsenal of weapons and anti-weaponry technology that the under-funded military does not have. The Republic appears to be locked into a civil war that is expected to be long, casualties high, and the outcome uncertain.

The coverage ends abruptly.

Looking up to regain my focus, I blink and do a small reality check; before returning my sore eye back to the computer, I realize that I must not be the only one who has read or heard the story. My swimming eye has not deceived me. The psychopathic guards have grabbed the warden and are dragging him down toward the black incinerator. Others are scrambling into the courtyard to get on the chopper to join in the fighting frenzy. For the first time, I begin to think that I will not die by burning in the peneteniary incinerator but in the cell by starvation and neglect.

This thought is short-lived.

The guards are afraid of the eerie but charming vice chancellor magistrate. They have left him alone and will most likely accompany him back to the capital where he will do his best to restore his twisted perception of order by assuming the role of the chancellor magistrate. I know this because he his walking casually toward my cell with two guards to carry me to the black kiln that has just devoured the warden.

I must enter the URL to my site. My hands are clammy and cold. I can barely move the mouse. I see him point his cane at me motioning the two thugs to open the door to my cage. I see them and attempt to steady my hands. Select All. Copy. I hear the key in the lock, twisting, reverberating through my aching head. Find story. Paste: Janet, Albert, Frank, Annabelle, Jonathon, Mary, Steven, Christine, Sharon, Jacob, George, Karen, Amy, Peter, Robert, Jessica, Daniel, Lisa, Karen, Michael, David . . . Their hands are on my sweaty weak shoulders.

'Make sure you take the computer too,' he said smugly. The gig is up; say good-bye.'

I am being lifted up, and the computer is being pulled from my hands.

Save.

'Why are we going here? I don't understand. It is not like it is going to happen again, and we have read and studied it every year since the victory fifty years ago. I think it is a waste of time and a clear case of administrative interference in our lives. We should have the choice to come here. It should not be a mandatory part of our curriculum. It is costly, hot, and far. We would all be better off if we were in class. At least it is air-conditioned there.'

'It will be cold enough at night in the cells for you,' the teacher said. 'I hope you brought enough warm clothing.'

'That is another thing. Why do we have to sleep out here? It is in the middle of nowhere, and we have to bring our own food. I think the whole thing is bullocks.'

'Well, you are entitled to your opinion. We will see if you still have it in the morning. Okay, class, get ready; we are here. Make sure you bring in everything from the plane. It will be leaving to refuel for our return trip as soon as we are inside.'

'Wow. Is that that the Arch of the Dead? It is much more ominous live than it is in the pictures. The shadow it casts on the entrance of the prison makes me afraid to walk through it.'

'Me too; my hands are trembling, and my legs feel week.'

'It looks like we are going to be walking into a tomb.'

'Yes, it looks much more imposing when viewed in person. It is one hundred feet high and has 200,500,000 names engraved on it. It stretches across the entire entrance of the prison to remind all that enter of the people who died here during the eradication of all the enemies of the Republic. On the arch, only one person remains unknown. Does anyone know whom that person is?'

'Yes, that's easy. It is the author of the story found on the computer during the civil war when the prison was used as a base camp for the military forces. Finding the computer helped launch a media campaign to win over more public support for the rebels fighting against the Internal Republic Security forces.'

'Very good. You know your history well.'

'I am first in the class, and that is why I don't know why we are here. I have read everything in the books.'

'Reading history books are important, but seeing things firsthand gives one extra perspective. Let's see if this tour can help add to your reservoir of historical knowledge.'

'On the monument, the assigned DNA number represents the name of that anonymous person. The interrogation room that we are about to enter contains the computer and the first print copy of the story of how two people, with the able support of a willing bureaucracy and a silent public, were able to carry out one of the worst mass murders in the history of the world.'

'I am surprised the computer and story were able to survive the fire.'

'Yes, it is quite remarkable, but the hard drive of the computer was protected by all the ashes of the prisoners who were burned after their execution. The computer was severely melted as you can see, but the inside was undamaged.'

'Can we touch it? It is amazing to be so close to an artefact of history.'

'Yes, but it cannot be picked up.'

'I wonder if the vice chancellor magistrate knew that the story would survive.'

'That is a question that none of us have ever been able to answer. There is no evidence to support the theory that he know that it would survive amongst the coolness of the ashes, remembrance was something he attempted to obliterate. The other speculation is that he thought he would win the war and the story would be covered over with ash and decay and never be found.'

'The next stop is to the warden's corridors.'

'It is so quiet and creepy in here. I want to leave.'

'Can I please go to the bathroom?'

'I am sorry; the only toilets available are the ones in the cells. I can open one for you.'

'What did the warden and the guards use?'

'They used the cell toilets too. The only cell occupied at the prison was the solitary confinement cell, so the administration did not think that it was necessary to put in more plumbing for personal comfort.'

'By the way. If anyone has to go to the bathroom I suggest that they go now because in the warden's office, we are going to watch a three-hour video compilation displayed on all of the still functional large-screen televisions sdepicting the unrelenting torture and execution of all the prisoners. Afterwards we are going to go down to the torture chamber and solitary confinement cell where all of the physical abuses occurred.'

'Cool'

'Vomit bags are located beside every seat and while the movie is on no one is permitted to leave the room.'

'Are you not going to sleep?'

'No, I think I am going to write instead.'

'It is a long trip back.'

'I know, but I cannot sleep. All the images and people are swirling through my head. If I close my eyes, I can see them. When they are open, they are also in front of me. It is as if I am there with them. I have witnessed all the atrocities committed to the one-and-a-half-million people brutally executed in this former Prison. Whether I am awake or asleep I am haunted by the same nightmare.'

'I sit here knowing that I can leave tomorrow. That is something that none of the former inmates could do. All they can do is stand boldly outside on a manmade memorial that serves as a tangible symbol of the honour and respect to all the people who brutally and horribly died within these dark and bloodstained walls.'

'Although an architectural masterpiece, the arch stands as an unsettling door into an ongoing nightmare like a real-life horror film that never leaves you. The smell of death is everywhere and cannot be erased. But after viewing all the films and reflecting on the texts written on the subject I am shocked and surprised that anyone would have permitted such a situation to exist—not only exist, but become valid legislation through an elected government. Like the grand arch outside, it acts as a timeless giant and reminder to what happens when tyranny is permitted to reign veiled in a delicate curve of harmless beauty. Merely thinking about it makes me shiver.'

'Reflecting on the prison and the policies that led to its reopening has made me realize that the only way for the lives of all the people slaughtered represented on the arch not to be meaningless and for their monument to be a landmark and marker that transcends time and space for all time is for me to promise that I will do everything I can to ensure that it never happens again. Then and only then can an open public space for everyone be assured, thereby allowing the many engraved on the arch be able to support their own weight to provide a large space underneath for the inhabitants to pass through going in and out.'

'I see that you understand the importance of the mandatory school trip.'

'I do.'

'What I do not understand is why anyone would willingly want to annihilate millions of people from the world because they were different.

It was a mad attempt to eliminate diversity and create a homogenous mass that could be added to or decreased from without any noticeable difference.'

'However, given the inherent tendency for variations in physical, intellectual, or attitudinal expressions, it is difficult to make everyone the same. Thus, when the initial purges of the immigrants failed to meet the policy objective, it had to be expanded to include anyone who stood up against the administration of the Republic.'

'I despise GT90347 for opening this place up and drafting the legislation that led to the murder of more than one million people. But I am also grateful for the protest, the Web site, and the story. Without it, we may all be ashes covering the computer and we might not have been born at all. GT90347 was an asshole but, by acting and writing, opened up the possibility for heroes to restore a space for people like you and me to speak in public and leave the horrible confines of these cold walls of death. That act needs to be acknowledged and thanked.'

'That is a profound analysis. I am looking forward to its inclusion in the assigned paper.'

'It will be there for sure.'

'You really should try to get some sleep. It is very late, and we are leaving early before the sun gets too hot.'

'I apologize for being so negative earlier.'

'Don't worry about it. I am just pleased that you have changed your mind about the utility of the visit.'

'Thank you for being patient and understanding.'

'Thank you for thinking.'

'Good night.'

'See you in the morning.'

'Wait.'

'What?' 'You really must sleep'.

'What is that?'

'This?'

'Yes, that.'

'It is just an old cane my grandfather gave me.'

'But'

'Yes.'

'You?'

'Yes'

'Sleep well my friend. We can talk more in the morning . . .'

BVG